PRAISE FOR JAMES SC

G000134659

James Scott Bell has produced gold in the Mike Romeo series, about a one-time cage fighter and certified genius on a quest for virtue. I want to be Mike Romeo when I get younger. *Romeo's Rage* was thrilling and moving. Highly recommended.

— **LARS WALKER, BRANDYWINE BOOKS**

A master of the cliffhanger, creating scene after scene of mounting suspense and revelation . . . Heart-whamming.

— **PUBLISHERS WEEKLY**

A master of suspense.

— **LIBRARY JOURNAL**

One of the best writers out there, bar none.

— **IN THE LIBRARY REVIEW**

There'll be no sleeping till after the story is over.

— **JOHN GILSTRAP**, NYT BESTSELLING AUTHOR

James Scott Bell's series is as sharp as a switchblade.

One of the top authors in the crowded suspense genre.

ROMEO'S JUSTICE

A Mike Romeo Thriller

JAMES SCOTT BELL

ISBN: 978-0-910355-60-5

Compendium Press
Woodland Hills, CA

How does a man know what is justice? It is not the product of his intellect but of his spirit.

— ALFRED DENNING

Justice delayed is justice denied.

— WILLIAM GLADSTONE

ROMEO'S JUSTICE

The guy behind me laid on his horn, his middle finger jabbing the air like an upside-down jackhammer.

Ah, nothing says Los Angeles like a fresh cup of road rage.

I'd been cruising along in my classic Mustang convertible, Spinoza, when this black pickup with monster tires tried to outflank me getting on the freeway.

When I did not slow my steady pace, he started to pass me on the shoulder. But there was a stalled car there and Truck Guy had to jam on his brakes and fall in behind me.

To this he did not take kindly.

He started with the horn, a custom blaster they could hear in Boise. In my rearview I saw him mouthing the letter F in various iterations and giving me the single-digit salute. He came to within an inch of my bumper, blasting his nuclear-attack-warning honker.

I remained calm, for I am a man of peace.

At least in occasional five-minute increments.

Road rage is a two-way street. The other guy—me in this instance—decides to respond in kind, and the heat gets cranked up. Sometimes one party produces a gun. It's a twofer if they both have weapons. There was an incident like that a few months ago at the downtown interchange. Shots were fired. One of them went through the window of a car driven by a schoolteacher from Monrovia. It killed her instantly. Her car veered into the adjoining lane and caused a three-car crash that sent two other drivers to the hospital.

I was unwilling to be baited into responding. I was on my way to see Sophie Montag and my mood was as sunny as the L.A. sky. I decided to end this encounter by getting off at the next ramp, letting Truck Guy go his merry way, then getting right back on the freeway.

But Truck Guy followed me.

I headed for Ventura Boulevard. Truck Guy stayed on my tail. He wasn't honking now. He was trying to make me sweat.

I turned left on Ventura. Truck Guy stayed with me.

He had the virus, bad.

Not the bio-virus that slipped out of a lab in China and brought the world to its knees. This is a virus of hate. It attaches to the soul. It's rampant, especially in places like L.A. It attacks the brain and shuts down rationality and self-control. It divides people into tribes that take directions from tribal leaders adept at controlling their mobs. When grouped, these moral zombies can lay waste to a city. Alone, unable to resist the hot anger burning in their cells, they lash out at whoever triggers their bile ducts.

You can only hope, if you run into one of these mutants, that they'll just get tired and decide to look elsewhere for fresh meat. Some have a girlfriend at home they beat up. Or a dog they kick. Some run for Congress.

But then there are those who are so all in with their hate that they play it out to the end. Every moment of their lives is a zero-sum game. Only winners and losers. To back away is to lose.

Truck Guy was one of these.

. . .

I went over my options.

I could try to outrun him in traffic, get some cars between us, frustrate him. But that would put other drivers at risk and I was sure he'd see it as a game he wouldn't allow himself to lose. I could pull over on the busy street and get out and see what he'd do in front of dozens of eyes, in cars and on the sidewalk. But those eyes had camera phones—everybody's got a camera phone—and the last place I wanted to go was viral.

Then there was the time pressure. I had a date that I was not going to miss. It was this consideration that made me turn up a street into the residential section. It was a risk. Maybe the guy had a gun. On a quiet street, he might use it.

But my calculation was this guy was more into submission. I went with my gut and pulled to the curb.

No one was around, at least that I could see.

Truck Guy pulled in behind me.

I watched him in the mirror. His door opened and got out. He was big. Dressed in jeans and denim shirt, and work boots that no doubt had steel toes.

He held a baseball bat.

I had an old seven iron in my trunk. I don't golf, but I was in a sporting goods store a while back and saw it sitting in a barrel of used clubs. Five bucks. A golf club's handy to have if you're strolling down a dark street. Your swing doesn't have to be perfect. Just hard and fast. But like I said, it was in my trunk.

I got out.

"Say what you want to say," I said.

He took a second to look me over. I'm six-four, 230. He was my height, maybe fifteen pounds heavier. Not all muscle.

"You gotta learn how to drive," he said. He slapped the bat into his palm.

"Granted," I said. "If I did something to offend, it was inadvertent. My apologies."

He frowned. "You talk too sweet. No respect."

"Look, friend, we don't have to take this any further. Too nice a day."

"We ain't takin' this anywhere. I am."

He took a couple of steps forward. Then whacked the snot out of Spinoza's taillight.

There's a Latin phrase from Euripides. *Quos deus vult perdere prius dementat.* Whom the gods would destroy they must first drive mad. This guy was far enough along that it wouldn't take much to deprive him of what little capacity for thought he had in his ugly head.

I know his type from years in the cage and hanging around gyms. You go directly for the male ego. You challenge his cashews.

"Wimp move, little man," I said. "Can't fight me straight up?"

He smiled. And gave Spinoza's bumper a whack.

I ran at him with a wild Apache scream, catching him off guard, but not enough to stop him swinging his weapon. I juked like a running back, ran past him to his truck. I jumped and gave a thrust-kick to his side-view mirror, breaking it off.

Before he could get to me, I hopped in the truck and locked the doors. There was a toolbox sitting on the passenger seat. I opened it and took out a hammer.

Truck Guy was at the door now. Found it locked. Looked like he was digging in his pocket for the keys. I hit the unlock and rammed the door into him. Truck Guy stumbled back.

I got out and faced him. He was ready to knock my head into left field.

I did a battle-axe throw with the hammer. Right into his chest. His arms jerked and he dropped to his knees. I met his falling head with my foot and put him to sleep.

As a car drove slowly by.

The driver, an older woman, looked at me with mouth agape.

I picked up the bat and tossed it in my back seat.

I went back to Truck Guy. Blood was pouring out of his nose. Grabbing two handfuls of his shirt, I dragged his body to the curb and left him there.

As I got in Spinoza I noticed the car with the lady had stopped half a block away, brake lights on. She was probably calling the police.

A good citizen she was, and that was more than enough for this situation.

I made a U and drove away.

"How was your morning?" Sophie Montag said. This was not going to be an easy question to answer. Sophie and I had come back together tentatively, like explorers in a dark cave who found each other again and were trying to find their way to the light. We'd been separated by my penchant for attracting trouble and raging against it. I thought I was better now.

"Oh, same old," I said.

I could feel Sophie's intelligent eyes reading me.

"That," she said, "is an answer Alice would have called curiouser and curiouser. What happened to your taillight?"

We were in Spinoza heading over the hill on the 405, toward Santa Monica. The top was down, the day hot and clear. It was Saturday and the traffic was heavy. People heading to the various beaches on the west side—Santa Monica, Venice, Hermosa, Redondo. Our plan was to hit the Santa Monica Fish Company for oysters and ceviche, then drive up PCH for the ocean view.

Both of us wanted a simple, relaxing time together. We'd had too few of those in the recent past.

But now this. I knew I'd have to tell her. Sophie was not a

prober. She wasn't going to push me to blab. I loved her for that, and for a lot of other reasons, too. The most important being that she doesn't run screaming from the room when I walk in.

Which is why I owed her that blasted thing called honesty. I never want Sophie to have any illusions about this piece of work called Romeo.

"Curiouser are the things that happen in L.A.," I said. "You know, you can be driving along, minding your own business, and some guy in a truck might take offense at your driving, and give you some attitude. That sort of thing."

"Sort of thing?" Sophie said.

"Well, that, and maybe a little more," I said.

"I'm getting the picture," Sophie said. "A bit of road rage, perhaps?"

"Right as rain."

"And you're okay?"

"I am, yes."

She waited for me to go on. Which I had to do.

"The other guy not so much," I said.

Again, she waited.

"I tried to get away from him," I said. "He followed me. So I stopped, got out, he got out, he had a baseball bat, and he smashed Spinoza's taillight. Then he was going to smash me."

A police helicopter chuffed over the freeway.

"They're on to me," I said.

Sophie said, "If they put you away, I'll visit you every month."

"You're a comfort."

"I take it then this guy did not smash you?"

"Correct," I said, and cleared my throat. "I may have smashed him a bit."

"Mr. Romeo, knowing you as I do, your definition of 'bit' may be slightly different from Merriam-Webster's."

"There was some blood," I said. "But not as much as there

might have been in the past. I held back. I just wanted to stop him. I did, and that was that."

Sophie didn't say anything right away. She looked straight ahead, her long, sunset-red hair blowing in the wind from under her Dodgers cap.

Then she said, "There are some things in life that must be accepted. Like death and taxes and Romeo doing what he does, before it is done unto him."

"Then I take it we can still have lunch?" I said.

"Of course," she said. "We can even have it together."

And so we did. Oysters, ceviche and tortilla chips, and a glass of chardonnay. Over which Sophie turned to me and said, "Tell me something about you that I don't know."

"That's quite a universe," I said.

"I'm ready to explore," she said, with the smile that I cannot resist.

"Any particular era?" I said.

"Is it too painful to talk about when you went to Yale?"

It always is. The wound that was the killing of my parents in that mass shooting will never completely heal.

Sophie touched my hand. "I mean when you went there. You were accepted at fourteen, yes?"

I nodded.

"What did you learn there?" she asked.

"Not to trust tuna fish," I said.

"Now that you must explain."

I took a tortilla chip and scooped up a bunch of ceviche. Sophie gave me time to chomp by sipping her chardonnay.

"Yale has a residential college model," I said. "Different colleges within the college. Branford College, Saybrook and so on. Each college had a master. That word is no longer used, of course. The language police won't allow it."

"Language brutality," Sophie said.

"My college, Branford, held a master's tea every Wednesday afternoon. An informal gathering at the master's house for students, with tea and triangle tuna fish sandwiches. The master would host a speaker to come talk and take questions. They'd be people who had succeeded in the outside world. Writers, poets, actors, musicians, TV producers, scientists. The idea was to give the college kids a look at what it took to make it. No prepared speeches, just an informal talk. Some speakers were well known, others not. The only thing was they'd all done well in their various pursuits. I always went, mainly to get the free tuna fish sandwiches. I just listened. Some students liked to pepper the speaker with questions, obnoxiously so. I never asked questions. Until one day an aging Beat poet came to talk."

"I haven't read many of the Beats," Sophie said.

"The celebrities were writers like Jack Kerouac and Allen Ginsberg. Kerouac wrote *On The Road* in what he called be-bop prose rhapsody. Ginsberg wrote a poem called *Howl* that got him hauled into court for obscenity. When the 60s rolled around, some of Beats went into the LSD craze which was championed by a Harvard professor named Timothy Leary. His motto was 'Turn on, tune in, drop out.' And the hippies were born."

"Fascinating."

"They thought so. Anyway, one of the Beat poets of that time was a guy who wrote under the name Jack Sprat."

"Did he eat no fat?" Sophie said.

"He sure gorged on the tuna sandwiches," I said. "He was a paunchy guy with gray hair and a pony tail, decked out in jeans and turquoise bling. And he went on and on about going *further.*"

"Further where?"

"He didn't say. So I interrupted him. I said 'What is the point?' A gasp went up from some of the other students, aghast that I, the kid, would interrupt this genius. Jack Sprat smiled. He was missing a front tooth. And he said, 'The point is there is no point. Get it?' And I said, 'No.' And he said, 'That's the point.' And all these heads around me started nodding. That's when I realized college education as we used to know it was doomed. Yale was originally formed to prepare men for Christian ministry. Now it's a carnival of nihilism and tuna fish."

"Now there's a header for their website," Sophie said.

A fter lunch we drove up PCH, the ocean to the left of us, past the Getty Villa and Mastro's Ocean Club. I turned up Topanga and we headed through the canyon over to the Valley. Got a nice, majestic view coming down.

When I kissed her goodbye at her place, the world suddenly seemed like *my* oyster. I'd never felt that before. Since I was a kid, I've always looked at life through the lenses of Thomas Hobbes—it is nasty, brutish, and short. Not that it didn't have its pleasures, like good food and good friends. Without those it'd be unbearable.

But with Sophie, a vision formed of the two of us on a sturdy ship crossing a turbulent ocean. Waters crashed against the hull, but together we were holding steady, and calm seas were ahead.

Driving home I tried to hold on to that vision. But another kept intruding, this one of wreckage, and me and Sophie holding onto a beam to keep from going under the waves.

I fought that one all the way back to Paradise Cove. And won.

It was a victory that lasted exactly one day.

O n Monday I drove to Ira's home slash office in the Los Feliz district. He'd told me we had a new client, a woman named Noel Auden, and a meeting had been set up for one o'clock. But he wanted me there at eleven.

Ira asks, I do. When I waltzed in I saw Ira in his wheelchair talking a guy who was standing. He was about my age and height, wearing a black T-shirt over black Levis. His body was hewn from rock. His hair was a mass of tight curls. They looked like if you pulled them, they'd pull back.

"Mike," Ira said. "Meet David Becker."

We shook hands. His grip was industrial steel. There was a tat on his right forearm, a snake with wings. Or maybe it was a dragon.

"David's the son of one of my oldest friends," Ira said.

"From Mossad days?" I said.

"Mossad?" Ira said. "What's that?"

Becker smiled.

"David would like to talk to you about Angelita," Ira said.

Angelita was a girl who'd been kidnapped and trafficked. I almost died getting her out.

"He'd like to hear some of the facts," Ira said.

"Why?" I said. I wasn't particularly interested in reliving that experience.

"Don't be evasive," Ira said. "You can trust this man."

"I just asked why," I said.

Becker said, "Let's say, hypothetically, that your child was taken. No ransom demand. Would you do anything to get your child back?"

"Of course," I said.

"But law enforcement has its hands full, and doesn't have the resources to help you. What then?"

"I'd do it myself," I said.

"What about someone who is not you?" Becker said.

"I'd consider them lucky," I said. "And then I'd find somebody and pay whatever it cost."

Becker said, "And what if there were a team of trained ops who did this sort of thing?"

"I would have heard of them," I said.

"Not necessarily," Becker said.

"Does such a team exist?"

"What team?" Becker said.

"Okay," I said. "I get it."

"Good," Becker said. "Let's talk."

I spent an hour in Ira's back yard briefing Becker on the rescue of Angelita and the other children, LAPD's response, the profile of the Guatemalan traffickers, and my own involvement—which included getting sliced with a *karambit* knife.

When I finished I said, "I hope this benefits your team."

"What team?" he said.

"Right," I said.

"But if such a team existed, hypothetically you understand, what would you think about becoming part of it?"

I gave it a moment's thought. It would be Romeo's world on steroids. Which brought to mind the part of my world where Sophie Montag lived. Going hyper-Romeo would close down that corner. I was desperately trying to keep it open.

There was also Ira to consider. We'd met years ago in Nashville, when I was fighting in the cage. I was walking down a dark street and saw a guy in a wheelchair surrounded by three teens, one holding a knife. I went over and did some damage to the thugs. They ran off. Of course, I didn't know at the time that Ira was former Israeli intelligence and could have taken care of his own business. But he was a rabbi now and did not want to hurt what he called "those kids." He scolded me for my intervention, but in a way that made me feel like he had my own welfare in mind. Later, when I needed to get off the grid, I came to Ira's home base in L.A. He took me in. Ever since, he's been my voice of conscience in the mad chaos of reality.

"I'd probably have to say no," I said to Becker.

"Probably?"

"That's what I said."

"Then the door remains open," Becker said.

"What door?" I said.

Becker got a laugh out of that one.

B ecker took off and Ira started preparing a tea service for our new client. As he did I browsed the bookshelf in the living room. I slipped out a copy of Cicero's treatise on friendship. Flipping randomly through the maxims I came across, *In the face of a true friend a man sees as it were a second self.*

"Ira?"

"Hm?" Ira said from the kitchen.

"When you look in my face, do you see a second self?"

"What on earth are you talking about?"

"Cicero says a true friend is a second self."

"I think one of you is quite enough," Ira said.

"I love you, too," I said.

There was a knock at the door. I answered.

It was a woman in her late thirties, with short brown hair and delicate, aquiline features.

"Hello," she said. "I'm Noel Auden."

"Please come in," I said. "I'm Mike Romeo."

I offered her a seat on the sofa. She sat and placed her purse next to her. That's when I noticed she was holding rosary beads.

"Mr. Rosen is making some tea," I said.

"That would be nice," Noel Auden said. There was a weariness in her eyes. She could have been a poet from the Hemingway-in-Paris years—seeing things deeply and forming melancholy verses in her head. She gently rubbed the beads with her thumbs.

"Here we go," Ira said, wheeling out with the tea service on the arms of his chair. I took it and put it on the tea table—Ira isn't a coffee man. He makes coffee only for me.

"Welcome to my office, such as it is," Ira said.

"Homey," Noel Auden said. "I like it."

"Will you pour out, Mike?" Ira said.

"Sure," I said, and began. There were three cups but I filled only two.

"Mrs. Auden has asked us for help concerning her son," Ira said. "I'm going to let her tell you about it."

"Would you start, Mr. Rosen?" she said.

"Certainly," Ira said. "Mrs. Auden's son, Steven, was a student at a place called Roethke Spiritual Center, down near El Centro. He had a single dorm room. Three weeks ago they found him dead in his room. A gunshot to the head."

A heavy silence shrouded the room. Noel Auden looked at her beads, her breathing labored.

Ira said, "Shall I go on?"

"I will," said Mrs. Auden. She took a deep breath. "I was called by the sheriff's department. They told me my son had committed suicide. They told me they were very sorry, and I could come down and claim his body. It sounded like instructions on picking up lost luggage. I suppose that's the way with them. They have to do a lot of that sort of thing."

She squeezed the beads. Her knuckles were white. "I went there and met with a homicide investigator by the name of Crowley. He said they got a call from the school. A student had been found in his room dead. That he had shot himself. That he had left a suicide note. I have the note."

She opened her purse and pulled out a single sheet of paper, tri-folded. She handed it to Ira. He opened it.

"May I read this out loud?" he said.

"Yes," she said.

Ira read. " 'I am very sorry for what I am about to do. I came to Roethke to find out if God was real. What I found out is that if there is a God, he has left the earth alone, and the earth is dying. And we're letting it die. Climate change is real, and it's going to kill the earth and no one is doing anything about it. I'm so sad all the time. I just want to rest.'"

Ira handed me the note. It was printed in a calligraphy font.

We sat in silence for a long moment. Noel Auden was trying hard not to cry.

Ira said, "How may we help, Mrs. Auden?"

"I don't believe Steven killed himself," she said.

A natural response from a grieving mother.

Softly, Ira said, "What leads you to that belief?"

"A mother knows," she said.

I said, "Is there a father in the picture?"

"There's a father," Noel Auden said. "But he's not in the picture. I got pregnant senior year in high school. Steven's father, his name is Jeff, wanted me to get an abortion. So did his parents. Jeff was on his way to a full-ride basketball scholarship at Ohio State. I refused. Jeff's dad was a big time lawyer and made it clear that they'd fight me at every turn over support, or would try to get custody of the baby since they were rich and me and my family weren't. So he offered to let me keep the baby if I'd sign a waiver, giving up all claims to paternity."

"Which is not binding in California," Ira said.

"Yes," Noel Auden said. "But Jeff was not the kind of person I wanted in my life. As events showed. He was accused of rape at Ohio State and kicked off the team. Last I heard of him was five years ago. He was a bartender somewhere in Oklahoma."

Silence again. No one had touched their tea.

"If I may," I said. "Is this in preparation for a potential lawsuit against this school?"

"No," Noel Auden said. "I don't care about any of that. I just need to know what happened. I need to..."

"Mrs. Auden," Ira said. "I'll have Michael go down and see what he can find out."

"I...don't have much money, Mr. Rosen."

"I understand," Ira said. "Do you happen to have a dollar bill?"

"A dollar?"

"Yes," Ira said.

"I think I do," she said. She took a wallet from her purse, took out a dollar, and handed it to Ira.

"This makes it official," Ira said. "We represent you now. This will enable Michael to operate in that capacity."

Noel Auden issued a relieved breath. Then wept.

We did manage to drink some tea—I forced myself—and talk a little more. The tea seemed to calm Mrs. Auden. Ira asked her for some background on Steven and how he got to Roethke.

"It was hard for him in high school," Mrs. Auden said. "St. Andrews has a nationally recognized athletic program, especially football. Steven was not athletic. He was, I guess, what you'd call a nerd. He felt like the odd one out all the time."

She paused and looked at me. "I don't suppose you know that feeling."

"Oh, but I do," I said.

She cocked her head.

"I was a pudgy, intellectual kid," I said, "and always the youngest in my class. So I know exactly what you're saying."

That seemed to bring her a degree of comfort. "He was very smart. I guess it was inevitable that he'd have to struggle with his faith."

"It has to be done," Ira said. "A child must grow up and make faith his own."

"That's the exact same thing Father Donovan told me," Mrs. Auden said. "Steven first said he didn't want to go to college right away, maybe travel. Then he found out about Roethke and decided to go there."

"You were okay with that?" Ira said.

She nodded. "One thing about Steven, when he gets something into his head he holds onto it like a bulldog." She didn't notice her lapse into the present tense. Or didn't show it.

Ira said, "What year was he in?"

"His third," she said. "He was only nineteen."

"What did he say about his experience there?"

"At first he loved it," Mrs. Auden said. "There was a professor there he really liked, who taught the history of Christianity. He left the school, and that made Steven sad."

"Do you remember this professor's name?" I said.

"Finney," she said. "Steven also liked the president...I don't think that's what he's called. Dr. Susa. But this year the tone of his emails changed. I asked him what the matter was, but he never told me anything specific. He just said he was having his eyes opened and had to keep looking. He was supposed to come home over their break, but he told me he was going to stay, that he had work to do. And then..."

She looked at her hands and worked the beads.

We walked her outside to her car, Ira using his braces. He'd taken a bullet when he was with Mossad and lost the use of his legs. Thankfully, he retained the use of his mind and heart, both of which he employs to keep me from falling into the abyss.

Mrs. Auden embraced Ira and thanked him. Then she hugged me. I felt the desperation in her trembling arms.

She was still holding her beads as she drove away.

"She does need to know, doesn't she?" I said.

"She fears her son may be in hell," Ira said.

"Catholic doctrine on suicide," I said.

Ira nodded. "The Catechism of the Catholic Church now recognizes that the conditions for a mortal sin may be mitigated by psychological disturbance, such as extreme anguish or grave fear of suffering."

"So I'm to try to ascertain Steven's state of mind?"

"That would be the place to start," Ira said.

"This is going to cost us," I said. "Have you seen the price of gas?"

"Let me worry about that," Ira said.

"Just don't worry about me," I said.

He put a hand on my shoulder. "But my boy, that's the duty I signed up for."

"Still?" I said.

"Just remember what the Book of Micah says. We are required to do justice, love mercy, and walk humbly with our God."

"Well," I said, "one out of three ain't bad."

"And just what does that mean?"

"I have enough trouble going after justice," I said. "I'll let you and the Lord sort the other stuff out."

Ira sighed. He does that a lot when I'm around.

Next morning, I took my usual swim in the chop off Paradise Cove. Nothing like the cold Pacific to get the blood flowing, the skin salted, and the mind prepped for a world gone mad.

I did a hundred Chuck Norris push-ups—that's when you don't push up, you push the earth down—then went back to my place, showered, shaved, and cooked some eggs.

I ate with my laptop open and scanned the website of the Roethke Spiritual Center, located outside a town called Morland, near the Salton Sea. On the home page it said—

Roethke is a spiritual space, a reimagining of where faith and scholarship meet, a forum for future influencers, a setting for solitude as well as gathering. We are an epicenter for social justice, quiet disruption, and a stillness that flows.

We exist for moral discourse in the context of multiple cultural constructions of human meaning. We seek to unlock potential hidden within our DNA. We build altars that work with the ancient elements to reach the essence of Manifestation.

I paused to listen to the stillness flowing from my manifestation, but only heard the quiet disruption of a little voice inside me whispering, *Oh, brother.*

I clicked over to the history page. It said the place was established by a man named Jefferson Roethke, a successful car dealer from Sacramento, after a "profound spiritual experience at the age of 59." He had a heart attack, and while in the hospital "heard the music of the universal song" calling him to the "cosmic connection of all things." He sold his dealership and used the money to buy a failed resort. This became the Roethke Spiritual Center, overseen by Jefferson until another heart attack "moved him to further research beyond."

I went on to the faculty page.

The purported dean was a man named Nicholas Susa. Only the page called him "Facilitator." He had a Ph.D from Union Theological Seminary in New York. His writing had appeared in *USA Today, The New York Times, CNN,* and *HuffPost.* His book *The Pursuit of Bliss: A Hero's Journey for Today's Pilgrim* was named a *Los Angeles Times* best book a couple of years ago.

A quick look at some of the classes brought up—

Wilding Religion: Re-envisioning Identity, Borders & Belonging.

Physics of Womanism.

Colonialism and Complexities of Indigenous Identities.

Situational Ethics in an Age of Plagues.

Christ, Praxis, and Truth to Power.

Well, at least Jesus had made the cut.

Another course was called *Earth as Abused Mother.* I clicked on the link to the course description.

> In this course we explore ancient traditions as they intersect with modern social and ecological justice. The course materials and discussions consider the ways these traditions, such as goddess spirituality/Wicca, polytheism/animism, eco-womanism, creation spirituality and deep ecology: 1) provide unique resources for the pursuit of justice and, 2) both critique and reinscribe systems of social inequality and violence. Students will explore the ways in which their own religious, a-religious and spiritual perspectives might more effectively empower them and their communities to create justice with both human and other-than-human communities.

I had some other-than-human thoughts and slapped the laptop closed. I finished my coffee, then went to the bedroom and started tossing clothes in a duffel. I wasn't sure how long I'd be, but thought three days would be it. Any more than that and I figured the hidden potential within my DNA would manifest itself by going bonkers.

Somebody knocked on my door.

"Yo, Mike!"

The voice belonged to Carter "C Dog" Weeks, the wannabe rocker who lived a few units down. We'd developed a sort of mentor-mentee relationship that we both enjoyed, which why it was not uncommon for him to drop by any time of the day or night.

I went to the screen door and slid it open.

"You busy?" C Dog said, stepping inside. His formerly rail-thin body was filling out nicely. I had him on a push-up and meat regimen in addition to getting him to read some good books. Body-and-mind reclamation from his former cannabis-and-junk food ways.

He was rolling something around in his right hand.

"I'm packing for a trip," I said.

"Cool. Where?"

"Around El Centro."

"Where's that?"

"Near the border," I said. "You want some coffee?"

"You got a beer?"

"Too early," I said.

"Not for the beach," C Dog said.

"Mornings are for clear heads."

"I'm so clear," he said. He worked his hand, creating a soft, metallic sound.

"What have you got there?" I said.

"Huh? Oh." He opened his hand, revealing two silver balls. "Takes away stress."

"Like Captain Queeg."

"Who?"

"A navy captain in a book called *The Caine Mutiny*. Humphrey Bogart played him in the movie."

"Cool."

"Or not," I said. "He was a paranoid who lost control of himself."

C Dog frowned. He looked at the steel balls, then back at me. "Man, Mike, buzz kill."

"Is anybody out to get you?" I said.

"What? No."

"Then you're not paranoid. Roll on."

He smiled and rolled the balls.

"So what are you stressed about?" I said.

The balls went *zhee zhee zhee* in his hand. "I did want to talk to you about something," he said.

"So talk," I said.

"I got a woman problem."

Zhee zhee zhee.

"What's her name?" I said.

"Dakota," he said.

"Are you in love?"

He shrugged.

"Have you slept with her?" I said.

He grinned. "Of course."

"But you don't know if you're in love?"

He doubled the speed on the balls.

I said, "Maybe you don't know what love is."

He frowned. "Can I plead the Fifth Commandment?"

"Amendment," I said. "Now, what is this problem you speak of?"

C Dog plopped on my futon. "She's crowding me, man."

"Mr. Weeks," I said, "this calls for more than just a morning chat, and I've got to take off on business."

"Can I go with you?" he said.

"Not this time."

"So what am I supposed to do?" he said.

"Remember when you told me you were a chick magnet?"

"Um, yeah."

"What did I tell you?"

"You told me not to think that way."

"Boom."

He looked at the ceiling. The balls went *zhee zhee zhee.*

I said, "All right. Here's my advice. Figure out if this is a woman you could spend a life with, or if you see her as just a physical convenience. Be prepared to give me an answer when I get back."

"That's a tough one," he said.

"Life is tough," I said. "You should know that by now."

"I wish it wasn't."

"If wishes were horses, beggars would ride."

A blank look. "Man, you make my head hurt."

"My work here is done," I said.

You drive in California by abbreviations and numbers. I took PCH to Santa Monica, caught the 10 going east, then the 60 all the way through Riverside and Moreno Valley. Back on the 10 through Banning and Cabazon, where they have the world's biggest outdoor dinosaur display. I waved at the pink Brontosaurus keeping watch behind a Denny's.

Further on, I passed the ruins of an old gas station. A bleached skeleton under the desert sun. You used to be able to drive the byways of this land and find gas stations where a guy would do the pumping for you. Also mom-and-pop stands and diners where you could grab an ice-cold apple cider or a hamburger shaped by human hands and fried in its own glorious fat on a well-seasoned flat top.

Now it's all pump-it-yourself fuel stops connected to a quickie mart. Eateries are owned by huge corporations, who alone can afford to cut through the jungle of federal, state and local agencies stuffed with cubicle jockeys who justify their existence by enforcing a tangle of regulations. If Ma and Pa Kettle want to start a restaurant in California, good luck finding a piece of land that is not home to an obscure species of snail under the protection of the Fish and Wildlife Service. Even if they could, there'd still be the permits and licensing fees, inspections and infrastructure enforcements, hiring rules and workers comp, energy restrictions and water oversights—not to mention lawyers, appeals, court costs, and money spent on anti-anxiety pills.

.   .   .

I stopped for gas in Palm Springs. It's a posh oasis in the Sonoran Desert, which battles the Mojave for the hottest spot in the whole U.S. of A. Somebody decided this would be a good place to build hotels and spas and golf courses. All they needed was water, which they sucked from the Colorado River. And boom, there it is, with palm trees, movie stars, and residents with cactus front yards.

As I was giving Spinoza his drink of gasoline, an older gent in a white T-shirt over a substantial gut appeared and said, "Nice ride."

"Thanks."

"Mustang," he said. "Had me one of those back in the day."

I resisted the urge to say, What day was that?

But he didn't move on. He had white stubble on his face and his jeans looked like they could stand up without him in them. Old cowboy boots on his feet.

"You heading south?" he said.

Instead of asking what business it was of his, I nodded once.

"I wouldn't do that if I was you," he said. "Here's where you want to stay."

The pumping was done. I put the nozzle back and took out a card to pay.

The old guy just stood there.

"Nope," he said. "Nothing but trouble down there."

I started thinking I was in a scene from *Moby-Dick*. Ishmael and Queequeg were cornered by a stranger in patched trousers who warns them about Captain Ahab and his wooden leg and who happens to be named Elijah. Prophecy, anyone?

"The land is cursed," the man said. "From here on down, cursed by the ghosts of the Agua Caliente Band of Cahuilla Indians."

"Well, thanks for the warning, friend." I started to get my car.

"Would you help a fellow out?" he said.

"You asking for a tip?"

"A tip for a tip, yessir," he said, smiling. His teeth were the color of dead leaves.

"Don't overwater your houseplants," I said. "Use a soil probe or a hand trowel to get a good idea of the moisture in the soil."

As I took off, I saw the old prophet in the mirror making a gesture that was a curse of another kind.

T wo hours later I reached the eastern rim of the Salton Sea —a landlocked, stagnant, polluted salt-water lake. The air smelled like gutter water carrying runoff from a salt factory. I'd heard people actually come here to float or even swim. If they don't grow a third arm, maybe that's okay.

At least there was a bit of blue on the right side to go with the desert brown on the left. Not much else. I did see a gaggle of black birds—probably cormorants—gathered on the shore for a meet-and-greet. That was the only sign of life, other than the occasional passing car, until I got to Morland.

It's a sleepy little town where the sleep is deep. Research told me it had one of the smallest police departments in California—a chief and five full-time officers. The Imperial County Fire Department provided fire and paramedic services, and there was a sheriff's office in El Centro for help with big cases.

Just outside the city limits, on a piece of property that can be called an oasis in the wilderness, was the Roethke Spiritual Center. If you wanted to get away from it all and steep yourself like a tea bag in the waters of spirituality, this would be a good spot to do it. I imagine John the Baptist, that Essene ascetic, might have considered the place a good retreat, so long as the dining hall served locusts and wild honey.

The Best Value Motel price was right, advertising $68 for a room. Made me wonder about the value of the other motel in town.

As I walked in I was met by the sounds of Neil Diamond's less talented brother singing "Cracklin' Rosie." He was a substantial-bellied man in a tie-dye T-shirt. He had a sprout of pink hair on top of his dome, surrounded by gray on the sides. He sang into a mic connected to a speaker, looking at his phone, presumably reading lyrics. Digital karaoke.

He made eye contact with me just as he sang to his girl that they had all night to set the world right.

He lowered the mic. "Practicing," he said.

"This place has a floor show?" I said.

"Nah, I sing on weekends at the park. I take donations anytime, though."

"I think I'll take a room."

He frowned and stepped behind the desk. He began tapping a keyboard. "How many nights?"

"Open ended."

"We don't get many of those," he said. "Here on business?"

"What if I said pleasure?"

He snorted. "I'd know you were wack."

"How about spiritual refreshment?"

"Oh, Roethke." He shook his head.

"Something wrong?" I said.

He shrugged. "Credit card, please."

I gave it to him.

"What do you know about the place?" I said.

"Why do you wanna know?" he said.

"You always probe your guests?"

He gave me a long look, up and down. "Just curious."

"Me, too."

He made a few moves, gave me back my card, and a card key. "105," he said.

"Places to eat?" I said.

"Mickey Ds."

"That's it?"

"We got a steakhouse."

"How good?" I said.

He smiled. "Sometimes the meat has marks where the jockey was hittin' it."

"I'll consider it."

"Um..."

"Yes?"

"Listen, I don't know, but..."

"Go on," I said.

"You really interested in that place, Roethke?"

"I told you I was. Why?"

"It's just weird, that's all."

I looked at his pink and gray hair. "Weird, you say?"

"Just a vibe," he said.

"Tell me," I said.

"I dunno. I don't get where they're at. I talked to a student once, at Jank's."

"Jank's?"

"A bar. He was talkin' stuff that was out there. Way out there."

"You remember any of it?" I said.

"It was stuff about Viking gods, and golden ships in the sky, some place that sounded like Impala."

"Valhalla?

"Yeah! What is that?"

"It's a Viking god meeting hall," I said. "Presided over by Odin, the king."

"I was raised Southern Baptist. That stuff rattles my brain." He shook his head. "Then there's that kid."

"What kid?" I said.

He put a finger gun to his temple and flexed the thumb.

"Tell me about it," I said.

"A student killed himself, right in his room," he said. "Doesn't sound like he was gettin' anything good out there."

"You think he killed himself because of Roethke?"

He shrugged.

"Okay then." I turned to go.

"Hey," he said.

I turned back.

"You need to be careful," he said.

"Why?"

"There's a vibe out there."

"Another vibe?"

"Not about the school. This one is there's people who don't like other people sniffing around. You look like you may be a sniffer. I'm just sayin', there's some bad dudes around who don't like to be sniffed."

"You have a way with words," I said.

"You, too, dude. Hey, if you're not busy Saturday, I'll be at the park doing a Sinatra set."

"Doo-be-doo-be-doo," I said.

"That's it!"

I put my bag in the room, then drove through the main drag. Past an auto-parts store, McDonald's, and the bar called Jank's. There was a diamond-shaped plaza in what could euphemistically be called downtown. In the plaza was a two-story City Hall, a post office, and an old-time movie theatre. Across from the movie house was a burnt-out building. A bit of sign remained visible—RUDY'S HARDW. It didn't appear anyone was in a hurry to rebuild.

At the outskirts of town I came to a stop at a road sign with an East-pointing arrow on it. The sign listed two locations— Roethke Spiritual Center, and North Algodones Dunes Wilderness Area. I turned onto a two-lane blacktop, its sun-baked cracks snaking every which way like so many varicose veins.

There was nothing but flat land on either side, though the northern part had some grass. I even saw a couple of cows.

It was 2:30 when I pulled into a parking lot outside the Roethke Spiritual Center. Here was a bloom in the desert, a collection of Spanish-style buildings with palm trees all around. Its former iteration as a resort was apparent in the wide and welcoming archway in the front. As I approached I saw the one-word inscription above the glass doors—*Further.*

The reception area was a feng shui showroom, all plants and earth tones and positive Qi. In the center of the space was a curved desk, wrapping around a young woman as if to embrace her. She was sitting, reading a book.

"Greetings," I said.

She looked up. She had short, black hair parted on the side and a ring in each nostril. "May I help you?"

"What're you reading?" I said.

"Huh? Oh. Meister Eckhart." She lifted the book and showed me the cover.

"Ah," I said. "The Dominican philosopher."

She perked up. "You know him?"

"A bit," I said. "I respond to his belief in processive reason. And his view that the just man does not possess justice, but rather *is* justice."

"Wow! Who are you?"

"My name is Mike Romeo. Glad to meet you..."

"Tomeka," she said. "Are you here about a position?"

"Actually, I was hoping I could have a word with Dr. Susa. Is he in?"

"Um...may I ask what this is regarding?"

"I work for a lawyer in Los Angeles," I said. "We represent the mother of Steven Auden."

Her expression went from perky to suspicious in a nanosecond.

"Not anything adversarial," I said. "Just a few questions to get her some closure."

Gears churned in her head. "I...can you wait here a moment?"

"Glad to," I said.

S he went through a side door. I looked around the lobby. On one wall were framed head shots of the faculty, all with ecstatic smiles. A potted saguaro cactus was underneath the photos. A hearty plant, the saguaro. Small birds make nests inside the pulpy flesh. It provides nectar and food, a desert cafeteria for mammals, bats, reptiles, and insects.

Which reminded me I was hungry.

Tomeka came back. Rather stiffly, she said, "Please come with me."

Nicholas Susa stood just inside his office door. I shook his hand. His grip was a good one.

"Please come in," he said.

He closed the door behind me. He looked to be in his mid-forties. In a sport coat and open-collar shirt, with neatly-cropped brown hair and tortoise-shell glasses, he could have been a CPA about to give tax advice.

He offered me a chair and sat behind his desk. His office was decorated in desert landscape colors—creamy whites, earthy neutrals, a few hints of green and pink. On his desk was a table-top fountain in the shape of a grotto, with two sea otters keeping watch over the pool. I eyed it as I sat down.

"You like my otters?" Susa said, his tone emulating the susurrant whisper of the flowing water.

"Sure," I said.

"One is named Wisdom. The other Serenity."

"Better than Rage and Violence, I suppose."

"Indeed, we have too much of that these days, right? That's one of the reasons Roethke exists."

"Thanks for seeing me," I said.

"Happy to do it," Susa said. "I mean, it's not a happy occasion, of course. So tragic. We failed Steven."

"Suicide is complex," I said. "Not usually one thing."

"Thank you for saying that. But we exist to help students find meaning and happiness."

"Was Steven one of your students?" I said.

"All the students are students of all of us, is what we say. But yes, he was in my class on The Hero's Journey."

"Did you know him well?"

"We try to know all our students on an intimate level," Susa said. "That's part of our mission. We aim for full, integrated, holistic relationships."

"That's some goal," I said.

"We reach high," Susa said. "Otherwise, what's the point?"

"The great philosophical question."

A little smile came to his face. "You're an educated man."

"I try," I said.

"May I see your ink?"

I held up my left arm.

"Vincit Omnia Veritas," Susa said. "Truth conquers all things. That's remarkable."

"The saying?"

"No, that someone in this day and age would have it tattooed on his arm. What is your background, Mr. Romeo? Where'd you go to college?"

"Yale."

"What degree?"

"I dropped out."

"Why, if I may ask?"

"Personal reasons," I said.

"Understood," he said. "May I ask if you have formed any spiritual beliefs?"

"Eclectic," I said. "Right now I'm sort of a Frisbeetarian."

"I've not heard of that."

"It's the belief that, after death, the soul flies up onto a roof and gets stuck there."

He laughed. "Humor is a good way to handle this journey we're all on. Maybe you should teach a class here."

"Be careful what you wish for," I said. "But I'm not here to talk about me."

"Right, Steven. Before we go on, though, I have to ask that you be up front with me. Are you here to gather information in anticipation of a lawsuit against our school?"

"Absolutely not."

"Would you be willing to sign a statement to that effect?"

"You're certainly careful," I said.

"We have to be, Mr. Romeo. What we're doing here is a departure from the norm, and few people understand it. We've had a couple of legal challenges."

"May I ask what sort?"

"Oh, parents suing to get tuition back, that sort of thing."

"They don't like the product?"

"They don't understand it, is more like it. I would never use the term *product*. Yes, young people come here and it does produce...changes. In our eyes it is a reformation of spirit. Some parents are unable to wrap their heads around that, but we are up front about our mission. There is no false advertising, as it were. We have not lost those lawsuits. But our legal counsel is adamant about protecting us."

"Steven's mother does not want to sue anybody," I said. "She just wants to understand. Needs to. And if you want me to sign something to that effect, I will."

He nodded. "Give me a moment, will you?"

"Of course."

He got up and left the office. I looked at the otters and listened to the water. It really was soothing. That's why I love my own water feature at home, a little something I call the Pacific Ocean.

Susa came back in. "Tomeka is preparing a form," he said, and sat again. "Maybe I can ask you a question or two as we wait."

"Shoot," I said.

"You work for a lawyer in Los Angeles."

"Ira Rosen," I said.

"Are you a private investigator?"

"Not private. I don't work for anybody but Mr. Rosen."

"And you make a living this way?"

"It's a long story," I said. "Mr. Rosen and I go back a long way."

"I see." He paused. "If I might venture to say, you look like someone who can handle himself in a physical fight."

"I abhor violence," I said.

"Nevertheless, I suspect you would make someone an effective bodyguard. Would such a position ever interest you?"

"I'm happy where I am," I said.

"But might there not be greater happiness on the road not taken?"

"We obviously can't know that unless we actually take that road."

"Which is adventure, which is fun."

"That's what the passengers on the *Hindenburg* thought."

He frowned. "Are you a cynical man, Mr. Romeo?"

"H. L. Mencken said the cynics are right nine times out of ten."

Susa steepled his fingers. "I can't live like that. To be open, not skeptical, is the only way to grow. If we're not growing, we are atrophying, yes?"

"Not all growth is good," I said. "Weeds are not chrysan-themums."

"But the journey is part of the reward," Susa said. "Joseph Campbell said that following your bliss is a risk. It calls for courage. But it's the only way to find your authentic self."

"What if your authentic self turns out to be a jerk?"

Susa cocked his head. "I don't think anyone's ever asked me that before."

"Seems we have a Socratic moment here," I said.

"You are really interesting," Susa said. "I hope things—"

There was a rap on the door and Tomeka came in. She handed Susa a doc, then left. Susa gave the paper a quick once over, then handed it to me. It was a release of any and all claims, rights, demands, and causes of action that Noel Auden or her legal representatives may have against Roethke Spiritual Center arising out of or in connection with the death of Steven Auden, including but not limited to:

Negligence, whether caused by the Releasees or any third party.

Breach of duty, whether statutory, contractual, or otherwise.

Emotional distress, mental anguish, or any other psycholog-ical or emotional harm.

Loss of companionship, support, or enjoyment of life.

Any other claims, rights, demands, or causes of action arising from the aforementioned incident.

This waiver and release agreement shall be binding upon Noel Auden, her heirs, executors, administrators, and assigns. It is understood that this waiver is a complete and final settlement of any and all claims related to the incident.

"Your lawyers sure know how to CYA," I said.

"What's that?"

"Cover your heinie."

He looked puzzled, then knowing. "Ah," he said. He held out a pen. I took it and signed the release.

"Now," Susa said, "I'll tell you what I know about Steven. He was a good student. Quiet. But something seemed to have made him unhappy. I noticed it when he came to see me once, to talk about a project. He was sullen. I asked him if anything was wrong, but he said there wasn't. He said he was just tired. But I sensed something deeper. But then of course it came out in the suicide note."

"Climate change."

"Yes."

"He didn't give you anything more?"

Susa shook his head. "I told him, if he ever felt he needed to talk to someone, not to hesitate to talk to our student counselor."

"Did he?"

"I believe so."

"What's this counselor's name?"

"Dísir."

"First name?"

"Just one name."

"She have an office on campus?"

"They," Susa said.

"Excuse me?"

"*They* is their preferred pronoun."

"Ah."

"Their office is off campus."

I felt like saying "Who's on first?" but thought better of it.

"Of course," Susa said, "there's doctor-patient privilege."

"If the patient is dead, the doctor can share voluntarily."

"There's the rub," Susa said. "I don't know how forthcoming they will be."

"So just to get a handle on things," I said, "how many people were around when the shooting happened?"

"Not many. We were on break. Most students clear out for a week. Faculty, too."

"You?"

"I was in Montecito," he said. "At Oprah's."

"Oprah Winfrey?"

"Is there any other Oprah? She hosted a summit of spiritual thinkers. Two days of awesomeness. And a PBS producer looking to do a series who talked to me about maybe being the host." He pursed his lips. "Of course, when the tragedy happened the offer was put on hold."

I nodded.

Susa reached out and touched one of the otters.

We listened to the trickling water.

I said, "Would it be possible for me to take a look at Steven's dorm room?"

"It's been cleaned out," Susa said.

"I'd still like to take a quick look."

"The sheriff's investigator already went over it."

"I'll be brief."

"I guess it'll be all right," he said. "I'll call the caretaker. Just a heads up. He's the one who found Steven. It really shook him."

"I can imagine."

"He's a sweet man, a bit challenged. Do keep it short."

"Absolutely," I said.

The caretaker was a man in his fifties. Susa introduced him as Eloi Kuprin. He was ample in girth, bald on top with a ring of unkempt sandy hair around the sides. He wore a long-sleeve shirt that strained against his stomach. Something that looked like a ketchup stain was on the shirt. His eyes met mine with wide unease.

"This is Mr. Romeo," Susa said. "Will you show him Steven Auden's room, please?"

Eloi Kuprin didn't move.

"It's all right, Eloi," Susa said. "He's a friend."

The caretaker's head twitched. "Um, okay."

To me, Susa said, "Let me know if you have any questions."

Eloi Kuprin walked with a shuffle and listed slightly to his left. He said nothing as we walked across the campus. There was a grass field where a couple of guys kicked around a soccer ball. Under an awning, at some tables, several students sat reading, talking, looking at phones.

We entered a dorm. I followed him down a hallway. At the last door on the right he took hold of the keys he wore on a retractable holder and pulled the chain. He fiddled for a key and unlocked the door. He opened it and stood to the side as I walked in.

It was a small room, a monk's cell, with a bed, a study desk, and a chair. A window looked out at the grassy area. New carpet smell was thick.

Nothing to see. The bed was newly made. The walls were empty and immaculate. The desk was connected to the wall. There was a reading light with a bendable stem coming out of the wall.

I turned to Kuprin. "You were the one who found him?"

His lower lip quivered. He nodded.

"That must have been hard," I said.

He nodded again.

"Can I ask where the body was?"

He hesitated, then pointed at the desk.

"At the desk?"

Nod.

"On the desk or on the floor?"

"D...desk," Kuprin said in a soft, tremulous voice. He put his arms out and lowered his head, indicating an upper body resting on the desk.

"And a gun?" I said.

He nodded.

"Do you know why Steven had a gun?" I said.

Kuprin's body shook. "Can I...can I not...I don't like to...think about it."

"Sure, sure," I said. "Thank you for showing me. I'll find my way back to Dr. Susa's office."

Kuprin's eyes were moist. "Steven...was...good."

"I'm sure," I said.

"I loved him."

"I understand," I said.

I went out to the grassy field and walked across. The soccer ball came my way. I kicked it back to the guys. One of them flashed me the peace sign.

There were two young women at one of the tables. They were both looking at their phones.

"Hello," I said.

Two heads looked up from the screens.

"May I have a moment of your time?" I said.

One of the two, dark-haired and slight, said, "Sure" at the same time the other, with nut-brown hair, said, "Why?"

"I wondered if any of you knew Steven Auden?"

Dark Hair said, "We all did."

"Everybody knows everybody here," Nut Brown said.

"May I sit?" I said.

"Who are you?" Nut Brown said.

I sat. "My name is Mike Romeo, and I work for a lawyer who represents Steven's mother."

Dark Hair scowled. "Is there a lawsuit?"

"No, there is not," I said. "And there's not going to be. We just want to find out why he might have killed himself."

"He left that note," Nut Brown said.

"Yeah, you can see why," Dark Hair said. She then offered her opinion that humankind was effing up the earth and nobody was doing an effing thing about it, "except the governor."

"How so?" I said.

"Only electric cars in California by 2035," Dark Hair said.

I nodded. "The extension cord business will boom."

They looked at me, expressionless.

"That's not funny," Dark Hair said.

"Neither is suicide," I said. "How well did you know Steven?"

Again, they looked at each other.

"He was kind of a loner," Dark Hair said.

Nut Brown said, "He was friends with—"

She stopped when Dark Hair touched her arm.

"Yes?" I said.

"Maybe we shouldn't say anything else," Dark Hair said.

"Look," I said, "I'm not here to start anything. It's for his mother. She's really broken up about this, as you might imagine. Anything you can give me to help close the matter."

"Maybe it's okay," Nut Brown said to her friend.

"Please," I said.

Dark Hair pursed her lips, then waved her hands in a *whatever* gesture.

"He was friends with Destiny Jacobs," Nut Brown said. "She's a student at Imperial Valley."

"Any idea how to contact her?" I said.

"She works at the Applebee's in Imperial," Nut Brown said.

"Where they serve meat," Dark Hair said. "We've got to get rid of cows, and soon."

"Eating them is one way to do it," I said.

"That's not funny," Dark Hair said.

"Tough crowd," I said.

"Don't you care about methane?" Dark Hair said.

"I don't want to be downwind of it, if that's what you mean."

"It's a potent greenhouse gas," she said with the seriousness of a preacher. "The livestock industry is a significant source of methane emissions."

"That really stinks," I said.

Once more they looked at me, expressionless.

I got up. "You've been great. Be sure to tip your server on the way out."

I went back to reception to thank Dr. Susa. Tomeka said he was on the phone and asked if I wanted to wait. I said just give him the message. She smiled, nodded, then got back into Meister Eckhart.

I thought about meat as I drove to Imperial. Winston Churchill prepared to save Western Civilization by eating roast beef almost every day. Who knows? If he'd been a vegetarian maybe we'd all be speaking German now.

I like to contemplate such eternal questions when I drive.

My thoughts became more practical when I got to Applebee's. A hostess at the front stand smiled and said, "Welcome to Applebee's. How many?"

I said, "I was wondering if Destiny is working right now."

"Oh, sorry," she said. "Destiny doesn't work here anymore."

"Ah. You happen to know how I can get in touch with her?"

"No." Clipped voice. Conversation over.

"It's kind of important that I find her," I said.

"I can't help you."

"No one here who can—"

"Would you like a table?"

"I get it," I said. "Who am I and what's my business? I work for a lawyer, and Destiny had a friend who just died. It's in connection with that. She's not in any trouble."

I took out one of Ira's lawyer cards and gave it to her. She gave it a quick glance, then set it down.

"I don't know anything about that," she said. But the way she said it made me think she knew a lot about it.

"Let me assure you," I said, "that anything you tell me is strictly confidential."

"I'm sorry."

"Can I see the manager?" I said.

"Um...he's kind of busy."

I looked at the half-empty restaurant. "I think he might give me a minute or two."

"Sir, we can't give out any information."

"Still, just a word with the manager."

She said nothing.

"I'll just sit over here," I said. I took a seat on the waiting bench.

The poor hostess was fighting something. I couldn't blame her. I'm not the softest looking guy. You have to get to know me to know what a pussycat I am. I picked up a slick brochure from a stack on a table.

The hostess left the stand and walked to the back.

The brochure was about the Temecula wine country. It listed, with photos, info about some wineries. A tour company had a few packages for sale. I thought about how nice it would be to go on one of the tours with Sophie. I was sure I could get through a wine tour without beating somebody up.

I pushed that thought out of my head and put the brochure back on the table.

The hostess returned with a guy about thirty-five. He had thick black hair and a Sam Elliott mustache. He was tall and in good shape.

He approached me, smiling.

"Is there something I can help you with?" he said.

I stood. "My name's Mike Romeo. I told your hostess that I work for a lawyer. We represent the mother of a young man who recently died, who one of your servers might know. But I guess she doesn't work here anymore."

"You mean Destiny."

"That's right."

"She left us last week."

"Do you know where I might find her?"

"I'm sorry, I don't."

"You must have her address in your files."

"I can't give out that information," he said.

"I can protect you from liability, if that's what you're worried about."

"Oh?"

"Or I could get a subpoena," I said, not knowing if I could. "That way it wouldn't be your call."

His lips tightened under his bushy soup strainer. "So get one. Now if you'll excuse me, I have a restaurant I have to run."

I didn't move.

"Okay?" he said.

"Thanks for your time," I said. "If you change your mind, I left my card with your hostess."

"Sure," he said.

"I am a bit peckish, though," I said. "How about a table?"

They put me in a booth. I picked up a table menu and studied the burgers. A server came to the table, a college-age woman with a ponytail.

"I'm Sheri, and I'll be your server," she said. "Can I start you off with something to drink?"

"A cold beer would be great. Tecate?"

"Sure."

She looked over her shoulder, back at me. In a low voice she said, "I heard you asking about Destiny."

"Yes?"

"It's about her friend Steven, isn't it?"

"That's right," I said. "Do you know where I can find her?"

She looked around again. "I know she likes to study at a coffeehouse called Bean There, Drank That, in Brawley."

"Can you describe her to me?"

"Black. Tall. Gorgeous hair. You'll know her if she's there."

"Thanks, Sheri."

"Sure, I hope—"

She stopped, looking over my shoulder.

"I'll get your beer," she said.

W hen she came back she was not talkative. I ordered a Bourbon Street Burger and onion rings with ranch dressing on the side. As I sipped the Tecate, Ralph started whispering to me.

I should explain. Joey Feint, the PI I worked for back in New Haven, before my cage days, used to talk about "the whisper of Ralph." Ralph was a "little man" that lived inside Joey. He based that on the insurance investigator played by Edward G. Robinson in the movie *Double Indemnity*. Robinson tells the slick murderer, played by Fred MacMurray, that a little man inside him tells him when things don't add up, when a client's story is not quite right.

Ralph was whispering to me now. He said the manager got to her. I told Ralph that much was clear. He whispered there was something more, much more, beneath this surface. I told him, Yeah, I know that, too. But what is it? He said he didn't know yet. I told him to call me when he had an idea.

My stomach, on the other hand, was in a jolly mood as I ate.

I paid the check with cash. When Sheri returned with the receipt she gave me a quiet, "Good luck" and was gone.

The manager gave me the stink eye as I walked out.

.   .   .

I drove to Brawley, thinking about what Ralph Waldo Emerson said about luck. *Shallow men believe in luck. Strong men believe in cause and effect.* I was somewhere in-between. You toss the dice and sometimes they come up 7. Other times, snake eyes. And all the in betweens. Place your bet—that's cause. Toss—that's effect. The number that comes up is luck or fate or a Calvinist God's predetermination. Who knows? But you have to play and hope you don't lose all your chips.

I rolled the dice by stopping at Bean There, Drank That. It was in a strip mall wedged between Rosie's Salon and an H & R Block. It was getting toward dark. A fellow with a white beard sat at a table just outside the coffeehouse doors. He rested a big pad on his middle.

"You got a face," he said.

"Excuse me?" I said.

"I draw faces," he said. "Let me do yours. Five dollars."

"No thanks." I opened the door.

"I'll make you immortal!" he said.

"One life will do," I said, and went in.

I gave the place a quick scan. No one answering Destiny Jacobs's description was there. I went to the counter and asked a guy in a newsboy hat if he knew a customer named Destiny.

"Sure," he said. "Usually she's here in the morn—" He stopped, frowned.

"Anything wrong?" I said.

"No, nothing," he said in a way that sounded like, *Yes, there is.* "You want to order something?"

"Sure," I said. "A large dark roast."

He tapped in the order.

"I like your lid," I said. Complimenting a guy's hat is a good way to break the ice.

"Thanks," he said in a frozen voice.

"So Destiny is usually here in the morning?"

"Don't really know," he lied.

I let it go. I paid and picked up my coffee.

Outside, the sketchy Santa Claus made one more pitch. "You got a Rushmore face. Let me do it."

"When I'm elected president, maybe," I said.

He chuckled. "You'd be better than the guy we got now."

Back at the Best Value Motel, I walked in on the pink-and-gray-haired crooner at it again. This time he was battering "Get Your Kicks on Route 66." His voice was to Nat King Cole's as a kid's kazoo is to Benny Goodman's clarinet.

He stopped singing just as he got to Oklahoma City.

"Hey, man," he said.

"Hey, yourself," I said.

"You have a good day?"

"Depends on your definition of good," I said.

"Good is good, right?"

"That, my friend, is a philosophical question."

He shook his head hard, like he was trying to shake loose an idea.

"Never mind," I said. "I got some things done. More to do tomorrow."

"That's always the way, isn't it?"

"It is," I said. "I never got your name."

"Troubadour Tim," he said with a grin. "That's my showbiz handle. My real name's Garth."

"Tim it is," I said. "I'll let you get back to your trip."

"Trip?"

"You're due, I believe, in Amarillo."

"Huh? Oh! The song! Man, I like a guy who appreciates the old songs."

. . .

My non-smoking room smelled like Bette Davis used to live there. You never get that odor completely out of the walls. I opened the window, with its view of the rear parking lot and the dry, sandy nothingness beyond. A warm breeze crept in like a nervous stranger, bringing with it a faint odor of salt and rotten eggs.

I plopped on the bed and called Ira.

"Reporting in," I said.

"Anybody get hurt?" Ira said.

"There's always tomorrow."

"Michael!"

I gave him a rundown of the day and told him I planned to see the sheriff tomorrow.

"Be on your best behavior," Ira said.

"Aren't I always?" I said.

Ira harrumphed. His harrumphs are always deep and full of meaning.

He said, "Anything to indicate Steven's death might not be suicide?"

"Nothing," I said. "There's a JC student who was friendly with him. I'll try to find her."

"Feels like grasping at straws," Ira said.

"It's what I do," I said.

"You tend to squeeze the straws you grasp."

"I'm getting better at it."

"Perhaps so," Ira said. "That girl of yours is doing you a world of good."

"I'm liking that world," I said.

"I knew you would," Ira said.

I stayed plopped and called Sophie.

"I'm in a cheap motel near the Salton Sea," I said.

"Business or pleasure?" Sophie said.

"The location kind of rules out pleasure," I said. "That's why I'm talking to you."

"Now that was a sweet thing to say."

"It happens on occasion," I said.

"How long will you be gone?"

"Not sure yet. What I am sure of is I'd rather be there than here."

"I'm of the same opinion," Sophie said.

"So...what is your class reading right now?"

"We just started *Romeo and Juliet*," Sophie said.

"How timely," I said. "Maybe I should give a guest lecture. You could call it Romeo on *Romeo*."

"I would love that," she said.

"I wasn't serious," I said.

"I am."

"Sophie, I'm not...I don't...I'm not much for speaking in front of people."

"A group of seventh graders is a good place to start."

"Terrifying," I said.

"I'll pencil you in," Sophie said.

"Make sure that pencil has an eraser."

"This is the strong, courageous man I'm seeing?"

"You are backing me into a corner," I said.

"Maybe you need that from time to time," she said.

"You sound like Ira."

"I take that as a compliment," she said. "Are you down there on a case?"

"A mother whose son may have killed himself."

"Oh...so sad. How old was he?"

"Nineteen."

Pause. "The world these kids are growing up in," Sophie said. "Suicide is spiking, and trending younger and younger. It's just awful."

"That's why you're where you are, Sophie. Teaching the kids, getting them into the Great Books. You're one of the few remaining Dutch boys."

"Excuse me?"

"You know, the story of the boy who puts his finger in the leaky dike, saving the town from a flood."

"Ah, yes."

"That's you, and teachers like you, of whom there are fewer and fewer. You're the real hero. You're the one with courage."

Silence.

Then she said, "Stay safe, Mike. Let me know when you get back."

"First thing," I said. "And you can write that with indelible ink."

I flipped on the TV and picked up a San Diego news station. There'd been a death in the Tierrasanta neighborhood. A woman reported that her husband fell down the stairs. He was pronounced dead at the scene. The anchor said, "Authorities say detectives are in the process of interviewing witnesses and gathering any evidence that may assist in clarifying the circumstances surrounding the incident."

Welcome to my world.

The next story was about a fight that broke out outside a school board meeting. At issue were a couple of books in an elementary school library. The film showed a group of mostly women with protest signs, set upon by other mostly women screaming their lungs out. One of the screamers grabbed a sign and ripped it. Another screamer grabbed the sign holder's hair and then it was pandemonium. Police came in to try to restore order, which is when the film cut.

That was enough for me. I switched channels until I got to an episode of *I Love Lucy.* Lucy was tromping around in a big vat of grapes, then started flinging them at the other woman in there with her. This seemed to me a metaphor for our times.

Then it cut to a commercial for catheters "delivered discreetly to your home."

I didn't even want to think of that metaphor. I turned off the TV.

I stripped down, got in bed and started reading Raymond Chandler's *The Little Sister*. In about ten minutes I fell into a dreamless sleep.

N ext morning I headed for the Imperial County Sheriff's office. Since I had to drive through Brawley anyway, I stopped off at Bean There, Drank That.

She was there, at a table, working on a laptop. There was no mistaking her from the description I'd been given. I went to the table.

"Excuse me," I said.

She looked up.

"Are you Destiny?"

Her face tightened. "Yes?"

"My name's Mike Romeo. I work for a lawyer. We represent Steven Auden's mother."

"How did you find me?" she said.

"No need to worry about anything." I pulled out the chair opposite her.

"I didn't ask you to sit," she said.

"I just want to ask a couple of questions."

"I don't know who you are and I'm certainly not going to talk to you."

I took out Ira's card and put it on the table. "Will this help?"

She picked it up. "I don't know who Ira Rosen is, either."

"Tell you what," I said. "Why don't I go order myself a

coffee. Do a search for Ira Rosen, attorney in Los Angeles. See what they say." I nodded at her cup. "Can I buy you another?"

"No. Thanks."

"Be right back."

I got in line, waited, ordered a large dark roast. When I got back to the table she had her laptop closed.

"He's legit," she said. "Sit down."

I did.

"What's that say on your arm?" she asked.

"It's Latin," I said. "It means Truth Conquers All Things."

"Why'd you choose that?"

"It's something I believe," I said. "Or want to believe."

"Want to?"

"I want to believe truth exists," I said.

"Doesn't it?" she said.

"Not for most people anymore," I said.

"You're very philosophical."

"My dad actually taught philosophy. My mom taught theology. What choice did I have? The quest is my destiny, which is ironic since I'm talking to you."

She laughed. "Nothing philosophical about my name. My mom loves Destiny's Child. She wasn't going to name me Beyoncé, but I could've been LaTavia or LaToya or Farrah. This way she got the whole group."

"You contain multitudes."

"I what?"

"Something Walt Whitman said about himself."

"The poet."

"You know his work?"

She shook her head. "Just the name."

"That's more than most people these days," I said. "Can you talk about Steven?"

Sadness took over her eyes. She looked at the table. "It's hard."

"Were you close?"

"I don't know about close. Steven was...reserved."

"How did you get to know him?"

"He used to come into Applebee's. He always asked for my table."

"Any reason?"

"Great service," she said with a smile. Then seriously, "I don't know. He seemed to like talking to me. I got the impression he was a loner, not many friends."

"What would he talk to you about?"

"Little things. Like food. Music. Movies. He liked old musicals, you know, Judy Garland and stuff like that. I do, too."

"Anything else?"

"One time he asked if we could have coffee."

"Was he romantically interested?"

She shook her head. "He just said he'd like to talk. So I finished my shift and we had coffee. He opened up a little about himself, where he grew up and all that. How he wanted to explore spirituality outside of Catholicism and ended up at Roethke. Then he asked me how I ended up at Imperial."

"How did you, if I may ask?"

"Nothing interesting," she said. "Getting my general eds out of the way. I didn't want to go right off to a four-year college. My dad's not pleased. But I want to take some time to find out what I really want to do."

"Any idea?"

"Culinary arts, maybe," she said.

"Nice. You get to eat your homework."

She smiled. "Maybe hotel management."

I took a sip of coffee. I liked Destiny Jacobs. She was so different from a lot of her contemporaries. She had a goal and radiated optimism. Maybe that's why Steven was drawn to her.

"The last time I talked to Steven," she said, "he seemed scared about something."

"Anything specific?" I said.

"He didn't say. He just said he was working on a project that could get him into trouble. I thought maybe it was something for a class. But why would he be scared of that?"

"No indication of what it might be?"

She shook her head.

I said, "Might it have been about climate change?"

"He didn't say that it was. I wish I'd followed up. Now it's too late." She closed her eyes.

I let her have a moment, then said, "Did you think he was at all suicidal?"

She looked at me. "I didn't think so, but there was a part of Steven that was blocked off to me. The only person he might have been really close to was a prof at Roethke he used to talk about. Finney was his name, I think."

I said, "Let me give you my personal number. If you think of anything else, give me a call, okay?"

"I will," she said.

The Imperial County Sheriff's Office was located on a thirsty plot of land on the southern end of El Centro. I parked in the lot and went in. A deputy looking young enough to be in high school looked up from a monitor on the front desk.

"Help you?" he said. His name badge said *Rodriguez*.

"I'm looking into a suicide that happened at the Roethke Spiritual Center," I said.

"Why?"

"I'm an investigator."

He looked at my Tommy Bahama shirt. "You have a license?"

"I work for an attorney. It's a quirk of California law that we don't need a private license."

"That seems a little odd."

"I said California, didn't I?"

He cracked a smile. "You have some kind of ID?"

I gave him one of Ira's cards and showed him my driver's license.

"What exactly are you looking for?" Deputy Rodriguez said.

"Might I have a word with the investigator who handled the matter?"

"That would be Deputy Crowley," he said.

"Is he in?"

"He is, but he's busy."

"I can wait."

"Might be a long wait."

"I've got nothing but time," I said.

He put the card on the desk. He pointed to a bench. "You can wait over there."

A s I sat, the deputy spoke on a desk phone. Then he put it down and said nothing to me. He tapped a keyboard and looked at his monitor.

Always good to have a book on your phone for times like this. I chose some light reading, a collection of humorous essays by Robert Benchley. I started "The Future of Man: Tree or Mammal?"

> The study of Mankind in its present state having proven such a bust, owing to Mankind's present state being something of a bust itself, scientists are now fascinating themselves with speculation on what Mankind will be like in future generations...We know what Man was like in the Pleistocene Age. He was awful. If he stood upright at all he was lucky, and, as for his facial characteristics, I would be doing you a favor if I said nothing about them.

I smiled at Benchley's prescience. Writing in the 1930s, he knew humanity was a bust. It was the age of economic depression, the rise of Hitler, and the Lindbergh baby kidnapping. If he were writing today, Benchley would hardly know where to start.

I finished the essay and was about to begin "The Sex Life of the Polyp" when Deputy Rodriguez called me to the desk.

"Follow me," he said.

He led me into the innards of the station and brought me to an office—a spare, square room with a desk, a filing cabinet, and a barrel-chested deputy around forty-five. If he hadn't been wearing a uniform I might have taken him for a Bekin's moving man.

He motioned to a chair and didn't stand or offer his hand.

I sat. Rodriguez left the office, closing the door.

"You work for Ira Rosen," he said.

"You know him?" I said.

"You bet I do. I followed a case he handled once. Defended a guy in Riverside who'd taken a shot at a deputy who used to work here. He was up for attempted murder, but your guy got the jury to buy attempted voluntary manslaughter, of all things."

"I know the case," I said. "It was before my time, but Mr. Rosen told me about it."

"A lawyer who can pull that off is pretty good," Crowley said. "Or pretty tricky."

"One man's tricky is another man's letter of the law."

Crowley humphed. "Who was it said the law was an ass?"

"Mr. Bumble," I said.

"Who?"

"It's from *Oliver Twist.* Mr. Bumble was a beadle."

"A what?"

"A church official overseeing orphanages and workhouses. The law charged him with being responsible for his wife's actions. He responds by calling the law an ass."

"How do you know all that?"

"I read the book."

"Wish I had more time to read." He put his palms on a folder in front of him. "Okay, I pulled the file. First, I'm going to ask if you've filed, or are going to file, a lawsuit."

"No," I said. "I'm only here to get confirmation of what happened for his mother."

"Why?"

"She's Catholic."

Crowley nodded. "I get it. What do you want to know?"

"How were you notified?" I said.

"Got a report of the janitor out there calling it in."

"Did you question him?"

"Yep," Crowley said. "He was plenty scared. But that's because he's, you know, not all there upstairs. Anyway, at the time of death he was asleep in the room he rents. His landlord confirmed it. He came to work the next morning and was checking the rooms for trash and linens. That's when he found Steven Auden. He called 911."

"When did you get there?"

"A little after eleven. Our ME confirmed it was a gunshot to the head."

"Was there a paraffin test done?"

"Yes. Residue on the victim's hand and wrist."

"You have crime scene photos?"

Crowley thought for a moment. "I'll show you one," he said. "But it stays here. If you want copies of anything, you'll have to get a subpoena."

"I don't see a need for that," I said.

Crowley opened the folder. An 8x10 photo was on one side, a stack of forms on the other. He turned the photo around.

It showed Steven's body on the desk, in the position Eloi Kuprin had indicated. A gun was in his right hand. Some books and a laptop were also on the desk. Blood was pooled in the gap between Steven's head and his right arm.

"What kind of gun was it?" I asked.

"A .38. What they used to call a Saturday Night Special."

"Untraceable."

He nodded.

"How would a nice college boy get his hands on one of those?" I said.

"It's not hard," Crowley said, "if you know the right people."

"Is there any evidence that Steven knew the right people?"

"Unfortunately, the right people are everywhere in these parts."

"Doesn't it seem like a lot of trouble? Why hassle getting a gun? Why not jump in front of a train? Or off a building? Or OD on fentanyl?"

Crowley shrugged. "A couple of students said Steven was acting nervous for a few weeks. One of them said it had something to do with global warming and doom and gloom."

"Would you mind giving me the name of that student?"

"Can't do that."

"But you wouldn't mind if I found out," I said.

"I have to mind. This case is closed, and I don't want to—"

His desk phone buzzed. "Excuse me," he said, and picked up. He spun in his chair as he talked.

I was into magic as a kid. I took the Tarbell course, which was a series of books on the art of prestidigitation. In close-up magic, one of the main skills you learn is misdirection. You get the audience looking over here when you're doing something over there.

And palming, the hiding in plain sight of something in your hand, like a card or a coin.

Or a phone. I took mine out of my pocket and snapped a picture of the photo.

Crowley spun back around.

I put the phone to my ear. "Calling my boss," I said.

"It's time to wrap this up," Crowley said.

I nodded. And said to my phone, "Ira, I'm almost done here...yeah. I'll call you back."

I put the phone in my pocket. "Steven's laptop. Where is it now?"

"We released it to his mother," Crowley said.

"Did you examine it at all?"

"No," he said.

"And I assume Steven had a phone."

"Nope."

"Doesn't that strike you as odd?"

"We think he ditched it," Crowley said. "Didn't want anybody looking at it after he shot himself."

I frowned.

"What?" Crowley said.

"Odd," I said. "Ditches phone, leaves laptop."

"The kid wasn't thinking straight."

"Yet had the presence of mind to ditch his phone and compose a note?"

"Just what are you suggesting?"

"Nothing," I said. "Just asking."

Crowley closed the file.

"I have a few more questions," I said.

He stood. "I've given you all I'm going to."

"I mean, questions for other people."

Crowley said, "Listen, I can't have you harassing folks."

"I'm an amiable fellow," I said, standing.

"Yeah, right."

"I'm not out to cause you or anybody else trouble," I said.

"If you do..."

"You'll run me out of town?"

He smiled. "That's a good old-fashioned way to put it."

"Then I guess that's the deal."

"You bet it's the deal," he said.

. . .

I drove through El Centro until I came to a 7-Eleven. I pulled in and parked. I took out my phone and looked at the crime scene photo. Something seemed odd about it, but I didn't know what. I do know that Ralph, the little man, was whispering again.

Everything pointed to suicide—forensics, the suicide note. And the fact that for it to be anything else would have required so many moving parts as to render it unlikely.

But unlikely is not impossible, Ralph said.

I already know that, I answered.

I went into the 7-Eleven for a sumptuous lunch. I scanned the buffet. Perhaps mini tacos would be authentic, as we were so close to the Mexican border. But I suspected they were shipped frozen from New Jersey, and passed. The burger selections were covered with wrappers, so it was anyone's guess what color they'd turn out to be. Pizza was a possibility. It's hard to ruin pepperoni, but could I trust the crust?

I was about to settle on a hot dog, which I could at least dress up with plenty of mustard and onions, when I noticed a guy in a hoodie filling his pouch with Twinkies. He moved on to the chips and filled one arm with Fritos. With his free hand he grabbed a large bag of Doritos.

And started walking toward the door.

I went to the counter and motioned to the cashier, a middle-aged man with a tired face. I pointed to the hoodie.

The man shrugged.

Hoodie was out the door.

"You don't care?" I said.

"Nothing you can do," the cashier said.

I made for the door.

"Don't do anything," the cashier said. He sounded like Ira.

Outside, I spotted Hoodie walking around the corner of the store.

I followed him. I watched as he sat against the wall and dropped his booty between his legs.

"I couldn't help noticing you didn't pay for those items," I said.

He looked at me with red-rimmed eyes. He was maybe eighteen, skinny. His hoodie was infused with the odor of ganja. He uttered two words.

"Now, now," I said. "None of that. Why don't you do the right thing and pay, or give it all back?"

He pulled out a Twinkie and clamped his teeth on the wrapper.

I snatched it away.

"You bite it, you buy it," I said. "Three bucks ought to do it, considering inflation and an inconvenience fee."

He told me what I could do to myself.

I grabbed a handful of hoodie and pulled him to his feet.

"Pick it all up," I said.

I let him go. He took a step backward and reached in his pocket and pulled out...a phone. He used his right hand to shield the screen from the sun and started thumbing it.

I was not about to be videoed, so I snatched the phone out of his hand.

He screamed like a stuck boar. He threw a wild punch. I blocked it, put my leg behind his, pushed his chest. Down he went.

Now I had a phone in one hand and a squished Twinkie in the other.

Hoodie scrambled to his feet and wailed. "Give it back!"

"Why?"

"It's mine!"

"See the lesson here?" I said.

He changed his wailing to moaning and his voice to pleading. "Come on, will you? Come on..."

"Tell you what," I said. "Pick up the food and take it back in, and I'll give you the phone."

He frowned, he blinked. His mouth moved, but no words came out.

Finally, shaking his head, he went back to his food pile and gathered it up. As I followed him into the store I dumped the Twinkie in the plastic trash can outside the doors.

The cashier looked gobsmacked as the kid dropped the stuff on the counter.

"Give the man three bucks for the Twinkie," I said.

"I got no money!" the kid said.

"But you have a phone?" I said.

"Come on!"

"And weed?"

"Whattaya want from me?"

"Look at me," I said. "Do you have money?"

I lasered him with my eyes.

With a defeated shake of his head, he reached in his jeans and pulled out a couple of crumpled dollar bills and some change.

"Put it down," I said.

He put the money on the counter.

To the cashier I said, "How much is there?"

He moved the change around. "Two dollars and fifty-seven cents."

I took out my wallet, removed a buck, and tossed it in. "That'll cover the Twinkie."

To Hoodie I said, "You hungry?"

"Whatta you think?" he said.

"Go get two hot dogs," I said.

"What?"

"You heard me. Go on."

"Then I get my phone?"

"Put plenty of mustard and onions on 'em," I said.

I couldn't tell who looked more confused, Hoodie or the cashier. Hoodie finally went to the hot food.

"How much for a hot dog?" I asked.

"Lemme see," the cashier said. "Five-forty-six, with tax."

I put down a five and a one.

"Why are you doing this?" the cashier said.

"I'm trying to deal with anger issues," I said.

He grinned. He worked the register, gave me my change.

Hoodie came back with two dogs in paper holders.

I took one of them. "This is all paid for," I said. "See? That's how it's done. A fair exchange of money for goods. Think you can remember that?"

"Yeah," he said. "Can I have my phone now?"

"Somehow I'm not reassured," I said.

I handed the cashier the phone. "Don't give this back to him for ten minutes."

"Hey!" Hoodie said.

I poked him in the chest. "You are going to see me in your dreams. If you steal, I won't leave you alone." I wiggled my fingers at him, as if casting a spell. "*Contra bonos more.*" Contrary to good morals. It was the best I could come up with on the fly.

I drove away, and realized I didn't have my hot dog. Didn't matter, because I was thinking about Hoodie, something he did. I kept seeing him shielding the sun so he could look at his phone.

That's when Ralph shouted.

I pulled over and parked under a tree. I messaged Ira the crime scene photo, and waited.

Five minutes later he called.

"Where'd you get this?" Ira said.

"From the sheriff's office," I said. "Tell me what you see."

Ira said, "Body slumped on desk. Arms on desk. Gun in his right hand. A couple of books on the left side of the desk. A notebook. A pen. On the other side, a closed laptop."

"Anything else?"

"What else is there?"

"The reading lamp, just above his head."

"Yes."

"Anything strike you as odd?"

Silence.

"What am I supposed to see?" Ira said.

"It's bent to the left."

"Yes. And?"

I said, "You position a lamp on the opposite side of the hand you write with. Otherwise, it casts a shadow."

There was a long pause.

"You think Steven was left handed?" Ira said.

"It's certainly possible," I said. "But then again, wouldn't his mother have picked up on that?"

"A good question," Ira said. "It's possible that in her grief and denial she didn't want to know more than she had to."

"Let's ask her."

"Before we open that door, let's see if we can confirm this," Ira said. "A reasonable investigator would have made that one of his lines of inquiry. Can you go back and ask him about it?"

"Um..."

"I don't like the sound of that," Ira said.

"I sort of took that picture of the crime scene photo...what's the word I'm looking for...?"

"Sneakily?"

"Surreptitiously," I said.

"Oh yes, that's a much better word," Ira said.

"Is sarcasm a Jewish custom?"

"It has come to our aid on many occasions, and now seems

apt." Pause. "I'll see what I can find out from Mrs. Auden indirectly."

"I'm going to talk to one of Steven's professors. My premise, until proven otherwise, is that we have a murder. That means we look for a motive."

"Michael, tread very lightly on this."

"I always do, don't I?"

"Like a mad Clydesdale," Ira said.

"I love you, too," I said.

I looked at the Roethke website again but didn't find a professor named Finney. I did a Google search and found a recent story on a San Diego news site about a professor named Roland Finney, formerly of Roethke, who was working on a book critiquing neo-paganism.

I tried to find an email or phone number for him, but came up empty.

I called Ira back.

"So soon?" he said.

"I missed you," I said. "Also, I need some help."

"That much is well known," Ira said.

"Okay, computer whiz. See if you can locate contact info for a Roland Finney, former professor at Roethke. He's the professor Mrs. Auden mentioned. The young woman I told you about, Destiny Jacobs, said he was close to Steven."

"You have been busy," Ira said.

"You get your money's worth with me," I said.

"Such a bargain," Ira said. "I'll call you back."

It took him seven minutes.

"I have a street address for you," Ira said. "It's in El Centro."

"That's where I am now."

"How about that?" Ira said.

. . .

The house was on a quiet street lined with palm trees and poplars and old-fashioned street lamps. It was a Craftsman-style home with a large front porch.

Where a man sat in a rocking chair.

I parked in front and walked up the path. The man appeared to be in his early sixties, dressed casually in a Western-style shirt and jeans. On a side table was a pipe rack with six pipes, and a tobacco jar.

"Professor Finney?" I said.

"Greetings," he said.

"My name is Mike Romeo. Can we chat a minute?"

"Come have a chair."

I sat in the other rocker on the porch. I felt like I was in a Norman Rockwell painting.

"Can I offer you some iced tea?" Finney said.

"No thanks."

"A good day for it."

"I have a complicated relationship with tea," I said.

"You're a coffee man?"

"I am, but my employer loves tea."

"And who would your employer be?" Finney said.

"Ira Rosen, a lawyer in Los Angeles," I said.

"You're a long way from home." Finney took a pipe from the rack. "Mind if I smoke?"

"Not at all."

He began filling the pipe from the jar. "How do you happen to come to me?"

I explained it all to him. As I did, he lit his pipe with a wooden match and rocked and puffed. I didn't tell him the theory that Steven might have been a murder victim. I wanted his take, if he had one, without prompting.

"Extremely tragic," Finney said. "I had a long talk with Steven last fall, before I left Roethke."

"Why did you leave, if I may ask?"

"It's like your relationship with tea," he said. "Complicated. Let's just say I did not fit there anymore, and some of the students made that plain."

"Let me guess," I said. "Something you said was, quote, hurtful."

Finney smiled. "Good guess. I was creating a hostile environment that made these students feel unsafe. I had the unmitigated gall to quote the Bible."

"The very idea," I said.

He smiled. "So God created man in his own image, in the image of God created he him; male and female created he them."

"How dare you," I said.

"I could have fought it out," Finney said. "But the battlefield has changed. Words used to be for exchanging ideas, and defending them, with quaint notions like evidence and logic. Now they are mere weapons in tribal warfare. We might just as well be grunting at each other."

He picked up a pipe tool and tamped the tobacco.

"Steven used words the right way," Finney said. "But was losing his faith."

"In God?" I said.

"In religion."

"Catholicism," I said.

Finney shook his head. "The green religion."

"Money?"

"Environmentalism. He was beginning to doubt the tenets of the faith."

"Can you expand on that?"

"Are you a religious man, Mr. Romeo?"

"I'm still thinking things through," I said.

"But you do believe in Truth, with capital T. Your arm says as much."

"Most people think my name is Vincent."

"Vincent Omnia Veritas," Finney said with a smile. "Of the Massachusetts Veritases?"

"Something like that," I said. I was beginning to like this Finney. He had a sense of humor like my father's.

"Truth and belief are two different things," Finney said. "When I was in college there was a popular bumper sticker that said, 'Everyone has to believe in something. I believe I'll have another beer.' That was me for a while. But after a dive into a dark abyss, I came out believing, with Augustine, that God made us for himself, and our hearts are restless until they rest in him. When one seeks an answer to that restlessness in another place, something else will fill it. Beer, drugs, sex, or a movement that palliates the soul. The green movement is a religion, with priests, prophets, commandments, and punishments. It is apocalyptic and evangelistic. It even has a holy land, a place we call California."

I nodded. "And the holy city, Sacramento."

"Spanish for sacrament," Finney said. "The irony is as thick as the governor's hair. And like many sham religions, it's a money-making scheme. It's driven by big corp, which has a huge stake in climate infrastructure upon which they expect to build future profits. So they buy politicians to kneecap free market competition by subsidizing the renewable industry, and strangling fossil fuel production by regulation. And then there's the new gold rush."

"Gold?"

"White gold," Finney said. "Lithium carbonate."

"For batteries," I said.

"For the coming electric car mandate," Finney said. "But this will require huge investments in new generating capacity. In other words, electricity, which we don't have the capacity for, by a long shot. There's more."

"That seems like enough," I said.

He laughed. "EVs are much heavier than gas vehicles. Did

you know that old parking garages are collapsing under the added weight? And roads, too."

"I hadn't heard."

"You'll be hearing more. The jaws of life can't be safely used to get someone out of an electric car. The battery is in the floor, and if it's punctured it can cause a fire or an explosion. The downstream effects are never considered by fanatics. Reminds me of the old Rochester song."

"Rochester, New York?"

"No, Eddie 'Rochester' Anderson, most famous for being Jack Benny's sidekick. He was in a movie called *Cabin in the Sky*, where he's tempted by the devil's son, Lucifer, Jr., with the beautiful Georgia Brown, played by Lena Horne. But he's married to the good-hearted Ethel Waters. And he sings a song about that old devil, Consequence. 'You want to sip honey while it's sweet. But that old devil consequence! And I ain't payin' the price.' We need that song again. Here's a consequence. The government will restrict energy use, thus lowering the standard of living across the board, except in the mansions where the politicians live."

"A religion that expects us all to become feudal serfs," I said.

Finney nodded. "Precisely. You know about the Salton Sea?"

"I smelled it as I drove down," I said.

"It's going to be a hotbed for lithium extraction. Several companies are getting into position. Which means, of course, money changing hands."

"You know this?"

"It's inevitable," Finney said. "There was that case in the Congo several years ago. A cobalt mining company pumped cash, loans, and shares worth over half a billion into offshore companies owned by a Turkish billionaire who was in bed with the president of the Congo. So the company gets mining rights, avoids government audits, and even has a judge or two in its pockets. The billionaire makes $67 million in risk-free profit."

"Nice work if you can get it," I said. "So you think that was the root of Steven's ennui?"

Finney thought about it for a long time. "I recall him mentioning one of the companies. FosterSynergisms. I don't remember the context, though."

I thumbed the name into a doc on my phone.

"There is perhaps one other item," Finney said. "Though I can't be sure about it."

"I'd like to hear it anyway," I said.

"Let me start by telling you of another student I had. Frederic Morrow was from a very conservative Christian family. What people used to call fundamentalists."

"I'm familiar with the term," I said. "My mother was a professor of theology."

"Oh? Where?"

"Yale, of all places."

"Fascinating! What did she tell you about fundamentalism?"

"That it was early twentieth century movement emphasizing inerrant Scripture and the return of Christ, and challenging Darwinism and German higher criticism."

"You are an educated man. Did you attend Yale?"

"I dropped out," I said.

"Ah. Perhaps that's why you are wise."

"I've been called a wise guy more than once," I said. "Now about this student of yours."

"Frederic, yes. He came to us from a small, private Christian college. He came under the spell of a professor who was a bit too zealous about her beliefs. This woman and I, suffice to say, did not see eye to eye on the role of a prof."

"In what way?"

"I believe a professor is here to challenge the mind so it will learn to think for itself. Her vision was, I gathered, to evangelize for her own philosophy. The sad part is my ilk is losing this fight. There's no longer a quest for truth on most campuses in our fair land." He took a contemplative puff, and said, "You may have to change your tattoo."

"I'll keep it for awhile longer," I said.

"Bravo. Oh, one thing more about Frederic and this professor. It may have had a sexual component. There were some internal dealings with it. Frederic never said a thing, but he left school shortly after. And slid right into an aggressive atheism."

"Aggressive?"

"Very much so. He started a blog that is robustly anti-Christian, anti-anything supernatural. Reading it broke my heart. I tried to contact him a couple of times, but he only wrote me a curt email to leave him alone."

"This professor, what was her name?"

"Funny you should put it that way. Her name used to be Chandra Klein, but she changed it to one name and a plural pronoun."

"Dísir?"

"That's it! How did you know?"

"Dr. Susa told me about her."

"Ah, Nic. I don't envy him his position. He's a gifted scholar and administrator, but has to oversee such nonsense." He shook his head. "I don't wish any ill will toward Roethke or anybody there. It's sort of like a beloved aunt who was full of life and love, who has descended into the dark abyss of dementia. She no longer remembers who she was or what she lived for."

"Is it possible Steven might have, as you say, fallen under the spell of Dísir?"

"I have no way of knowing. But it makes me sad to think it is not out of the realm of possibility."

"If I wanted to get in touch with this Frederic, how would I do it?"

"I have his email address, but he won't answer."

"No idea where he lives?"

"Here in El Centro someplace. He has a PO box. It's on his

website. You can look it up for yourself. CamusForever dot com. I guess he's found his home in French Existentialism."

"The paradox of the absurd."

"By Jove, I like talking to you. Are you in town long?"

"As long as it takes," I said.

"Please feel free to drop by again," he said. "I'm starved for conversations like this."

I knew what he meant. I was lucky to have Ira and Sophie to kick around ideas with. There weren't a lot of deep conversations going on in the public square. People seem unable to think in units over 280 characters. And most of those characters are taken up by emotion, vitriol, cursing and howling at the moon. A far cry from the Federalist Papers or the Lincoln-Douglas debates. Technologically, America has advanced. Cognitively, it is regressing back to the Stone Age. We are becoming a society of grunts and clubs, of throwing rocks and dancing wildly around the campfire, which is often a police car set ablaze.

Which made me all the more curious to find out what this counselor, Dísir, was peddling. Her office was in a modest professional building in Brawley.

I went into a small reception area. A young woman at the desk looked up from her computer. She stood out in that there was nothing about her that stood out. She had no markings or piercings or color streaks in her blond hair. She could have been the proverbial girl next door in an old Mickey Rooney movie.

I said, "I wonder if I might have a word with the counselor."

"May I ask what it's regarding?" she said.

I handed her Ira's card. "We represent the mother of Steven Auden. I understand he was in counseling here."

She gave the card a hard look, then transferred the look to me.

"You're a lawyer?" she said.

"Just work for one," I said.

"You know we cannot give out patient information."

"Unless the patient is dead," I said. "A mother can make the request and I am here on behalf of the mother."

The receptionist took a quick look at her monitor. "I'm afraid they are all tied up today."

"Who is?"

"Dísir."

"Shouldn't that be they is tied up?"

"Excuse me?"

"Their preferred pronoun refers to a single person."

She squinted. "I don't know what you mean. But I'm sorry, they can't see you."

"She...they...will want to see me."

"But I've told you—"

"I can wait."

Her jaw muscles tightened. She picked up the handset on a desk phone and pressed a button.

"Sorry to disturb you," she said, "but there's a man out here who refuses to leave unless he talks to you....It's about Steven Auden....I don't know...all right."

She replaced the handset and looked at me, not saying a word.

The side door opened and Dísir blew through it. She...they...was on the small side, dressed in tight black pants and a tight black shirt that showed, at least in the old way of figuring things, the dimensions of a woman. Her long hair was black with a sky-blue streak that ran down one side. Her nose was aquiline.

"Who are you?" she said.

"My name is Mike Romeo. I work for a lawyer in L.A. We represent Steven Auden's mother."

"There's nothing I can tell you," Dísir said. "Surely you know that."

"He's dead," I said. "Surely you know *that*."

She stiffened.

"We could hash this out in court," I said.

"Try it," Dísir said.

"You going to call down the god of thunder?"

Her eyes widened.

I said, "Isn't a dísir a female spirit associated with Fate who acts as a protective spirit of Norse clans? Who might have an in with Odin and Thor?"

"You're very flippant," Dísir said.

"We just want to find out what Steven's state of mind was. Can you tell us anything at all?"

She gave me a long, inspective look, like a hawk on top of a barn eyeing the chickens.

"That information is privileged," she said.

"The patient is dead," I said. "You can disclose information to relatives or their representatives."

"All I will tell you is that Steven was very much struggling with anxiety. Looping feelings of tension, troubled thoughts, and increased blood pressure."

"What was he anxious about?"

"That's asking for too many details," Dísir said. "I will, however, offer you just one. He was quite troubled about the environment."

"That much was in his note," I said.

"All right, then."

"Did he ever mention any names to you?" I said. "People he may have had some trouble with?"

"I'm not going to tell you anything else."

"Just one more question—"

"Did you not hear me?" Dísir said.

"Like Thor's hammer," I said.

She turned and went back from whence she had come.

. . .

The day was fading away. I decided to drop by the watering hole Troubadour Tim told me about.

Jank's was a bar of the last chance variety, a place you came to drink yourself into a nightly stupor. An odor like dead plants soaked in Schlitz filled the place. Four men sat at one end of the bar. They were all north of sixty and were having an animated conversation about something. I could tell by the flapping of their arms. I went to a stool at the other end and waited for the bartender.

He saw me and came over. He was a wiry guy of about forty, with thick brown hair secured in a ponytail.

"Afternoon," he said.

"Howdy," I said.

"What can I get you?"

"If I order a beer, can you give me a little conversation?"

"It's what I'm good at," he said.

"Corona," I said.

He went to a cooler and pulled out a long neck. He popped the cap with an opener and came back, setting the bottle in front of me.

"Lime wedge?" I asked.

"You know the price of limes these days?" he said. "If you can find 'em, that is."

"Price of everything," I said.

"You got that right," he said. "You from around here?"

"L.A.," I said.

His face lit up. "That's where I'm headed."

"Yeah?"

"Soon as I sell my mom's house, I'm moving up there."

"With your mom?"

"No, she died. Left me the house. If only she died a year ago."

"Excuse me?"

"She was gone anyway. Alzheimer's. You know what that's like?"

"Not first hand," I said.

"It's hell," he said. "Not knowing me, the kid she brought into the world and raised up and took care of when he was sick." He pointed to his eyes. "Nothing there. No reason for it to drag on and on." He paused, shook his head. "And a year ago real estate was booming. I coulda got half a mil for the house, like that." He snapped his fingers. "Now I got to price it under four, and there's no offers. None. Zip."

"What'll you do in L.A.?" I said

"Direct," he said. "I'm gonna make movies. Horror movies. Lots of blood."

"Cheery," I said.

"Get people's minds off the real horror, which is now."

"No argument there."

One of the guys at the other end said, "Tommy, fill me up."

"Excuse me," Tommy said, and went off to do his bartending duty.

I took a sip of my limeless Corona, which is like eating an egg without salt. A new guy entered the bar and went over to the four guys at the end. He was more my age, with a bald dome and a goatee. He was also rock-muscled, like a serious workout guy —or a former hard-time prisoner. He took the last stool at the L-shaped bar, which gave him a direct sight line to me.

Which he used to give me a look. The kind that says, *You know I'm looking at you, what're you gonna do about it?*

He said something to Tommy, then the other guys, and the group convo started up again. Tommy poured a couple of drinks, then came back my way. He plopped a towel on the bar top and rubbed it around.

"So," Tommy said, "what brings you to our town?"

"A little business," I said.

He snorted. "In Morland?"

"Is that so strange?" I said.

"Yeah, it is," Tommy said. "What business could it be?"

"I'm a spiritual seeker," I said.

"A what?"

"I understand there's a spiritual center around these parts," I said.

He rolled his eyes.

"You know about it?" I said.

"Sure," he said.

"What do you know?" I said.

"What do you mean, what do I know?"

"You're a bartender," I said. "You hear things."

He shrugged. "A bunch of navel gazers. Are you really interested in that stuff?"

"I am," I said.

"What do you do in L.A.?"

I smiled. "Tell you what. Why don't you go ahead and ask your buddy to come down here and question me himself?"

"What? I don't know—"

"He asked you to pump me, didn't he?"

"Look man, I don't know—" Tommy looked to the end of the bar.

Goatee got up and walked over to where I was sitting. He had dark blue tats on his neck. "What's your deal?" he said.

"I have a deal?" I said.

"You're in here for something. Why don't you tell me what it is?"

Tommy said, "It's about that freak college."

Goatee put his hand up to silence Tommy. He nodded toward the far end of the bar. Tommy headed there.

"What's your interest?" Goatee said.

"I have many," I said.

"Such as?"

"Gardening, macramé."

"Don't mess with me," he said.

"I'm serious about the gardening," I said.

"I mean your interest around here," he said.

"What's *your* interest?" I said.

"I'm the one who's asking."

"Who are you to be asking anything?" I said.

"Want me to show you?" he said.

"Anything to move this conversation along," I said.

He poked me in the shoulder. And smiled.

"That's it?" I said.

"Wanna do something about it?" he said.

"Really? You want to be a cliché?"

"A what?"

"Have a bar fight? That's been done to death."

He palmed me in the shoulder, hard.

"I guess so," I said.

As I slid off the barstool, Goatee tried to cold-cock me. I was ready, though, and ducked it. I gave him Romeo's Hammer, my right fist, into his breadbasket. He had hard abs, but the Hammer doubled him over. I put my hand on the back of his head and slammed it on the bar so hard my Corona fell over.

Goatee fell to the floor. Blood flowed from his exquisitely broken nose.

"Hey hey hey!" Tommy came flying back, waving his hands, as the oldsters made various sounds of disapproval.

"What gives around here?" I said. "Who is this clown?"

"You better get out now," Tommy said, "or you're a dead man."

"More clichés?" I said. "Dialogue like that isn't going to sell a screenplay."

"Get out!"

"What do I owe you for the beer?"

"Just leave."

Goatee was still groggy on the floor. I dug out a ten and put it on the bar. "A little extra for the cleanup," I said.

I stepped over Goatee and walked out.

I drove away tired. Tired of the road rage guys, the bar fight guys. There's always more of them. History is about one thing, and has been ever since hunter clubbed gatherer and took his berries.

Conquest.

It's always been about beating the other guys into submission. From the Greeks and Romans to mobs on a city street. Destroy and dominate.

The Spartans understood this better than anybody. From age seven the boys were trained to fight. It was fight or be conquered. There was no sitting it out. After a battle you came back with your shield, or on it.

I still had my shield.

That's what I was thinking in the short drive back to my motel. Sometimes I wish I could just think about my flowers. But there are weeds in every garden, and you don't reason with weeds. You rip them out.

In my room, I took a look at the CamusForever website and read a few blog entries. It was all warmed-over Richard Dawkins, who is warmed-over Robert Ingersoll, who is warmed-over Voltaire. There are no original ideas in atheism, only variations on a theme.

This site had a whole lot of variations. Including Camus himself, an existentialist who denied being an existentialist, in a perfect example of the absurd begetting the absurd.

On the "About" page there was a photo of Frederic. He had his arms crossed and glared at the camera, a take-on-all-comers look. With the arrogance of youth he was ready to take on the entire history of religious thought. And why not? There are teenagers on TikTok who fancy themselves smarter than Plato and wiser than Socrates. They can explain life in thirty seconds and millions will like it. Think of all the money we can save now by not printing books.

I took note of the PO box on the contact page.

A search found a UPS store in El Centro. It'd be a stretch to think I could stake the place out and find the guy. But at this point I needed a stretch. I needed to find something to grab onto. I hate the feeling that there's something there, but you can't quite see it, like one of those 3D paintings you're supposed to look at until it shows you a picture of a rocket ship or Abraham Lincoln.

That night I dreamed of swirling dots, to the sound of someone laughing.

N ext morning, I drove through Mickey Ds and picked up a sumptuous sausage-and-egg McMuffin and a large coffee. Ate and sipped down to El Centro. The UPS store was between a nail salon and a taco eatery. The ubiquitous, green oasis of Starbucks was nearby.

Stakeouts are notoriously boring and taxing to the bladder. Joey Feint always brought an empty milk jug with him for nature's call. He used it once when I went on a stakeout with him. I turned my head as he demonstrated his, um, flexibility. "You can't sit and see if you have to pee," he said. Words of wisdom I have not forgotten.

Only I didn't have a jug with me.

I got out and went to the UPS store and looked in the window. Nobody in there except a woman behind the counter. I saw the row of boxes to the left. I ducked into Starbucks and ordered a dark roast and took care of my immediate concern. I picked up my coffee and gave another look inside the UPS store.

Just the clerk. I got back in Spinoza and found a classical station on the radio. They were playing Gershwin's "Rhapsody in Blue."

Over the next hour several people went in and out of the UPS store, none of them my mark.

I listened to Dvorak's "New World Symphony," and selections from Chopin and Mendelssohn. In the middle of Aaron Copland's "Appalachian Spring" I spotted Frederic going into the store.

I followed. When I got in Frederic was looking in his box, then snapped it closed. Apparently his cupboard was bare.

"Frederic?"

He whipped around.

"Can we talk a minute?" I said.

"Who are you?"

"It's about the situation at Roethke," I said.

He gave me an atheist's skeptical squint. "How did you find me?"

"Visited your website," I said. "This is where your box is."

"You staked me out?"

"I can explain," I said. "There's nothing sinister here. Just a few questions and I'm gone."

"Questions about what?"

"You want to do this here?"

He looked around. "No."

"There's tables at Starbucks. Give me two minutes. That's all."

"Why should I?" he said.

"A hundred and twenty seconds," I said. "Then you can send me on my way if you want. I think you'll be interested."

His mind churned for a moment. "Two minutes."

We walked to Starbucks and sat at a table under a green umbrella. An old man who looked like he hadn't washed in a week sat at another table, staring. He had no coffee cup in front of him.

"All right," Frederic said. "Go."

"It's about that student at Roethke who died," I said.

"Yeah," Frederic said. "Blasted his own head. "All 'cause he was so upset about the earth." He shook his head. "They really messed him up."

"Who?" I said.

"The wack jobs at Roethke. They're all climate crazy, especially the chicks."

"I take it you're not married," I said.

"No way, not with what you have to choose from these days. There's no reasoning with 'em. Doesn't matter if you have the facts, they just want to cry about CO_2 and polar bears. Fools don't know they're just making everything worse."

"Oh?"

"Of course, don't you read?"

"Sometimes. I like *The Hardy Boys.*"

He went on as if I'd said nothing. "Look, even if we did everything they want, it only, at best, makes us point-oh-five degrees cooler by 2100. That's a rounding error, man. Meanwhile, all the manufacturing they shut down here moves to China, who's building more coal plants than you can count, and CO_2 keeps going up, up, up. And when you tell 'em to go nuclear, their freaking eyes glaze over because their brainwashed brains won't allow anything in that their overlords tell them not to think about."

"But you, you're a thinker," I said.

"You got that right," he said. "So this little snowflake can't take it anymore and shoots himself."

"You really have the milk of human kindness flowing."

"What good does that do anybody? The kid was a coward."

"Coward?"

"You don't just check out," he said. "Life's absurd but you gotta face it."

"Camus Forever, huh?"

His mouth creased into a smile. "You get it, don't you?"

"No," I said.

"What don't you get?"

"You want my opinion?" I said.

"Sure, why not?"

"Will this be deducted from my two minutes?"

He folded his arms like in his website photo. "No."

"Existentialism is just atheism in a cheap tuxedo," I said.

His chin fell about four stories.

"And dogmatic atheism," I said, "is irrational."

That brought out the growling dog in him. "Belief in God is what's irrational! Might as well believe in the Tooth Fairy."

"The Tooth Fairy does not have millions of credible witnesses," I said. "Surely you've read James's *The Varieties of Religious Experience.*"

"Who?"

"William James," I said. "Tell you what, you read it and we'll have another conversation."

"Not likely," he said.

"Then start my two minutes," I said.

He looked at his watch. "Go."

"I work for a lawyer representing Steven Auden's mother. We're gathering information."

"What are you talking to me for?"

"I spoke to your former professor, Roland Finney."

His jaw muscles tightened, like he was clamping down on beef jerky. "So?"

"He's rather fond of you," I said.

"He's a dinosaur," Frederic said.

"He told me something about you, and there may be a connection that can help me with the dots I'm trying to connect."

"Like what?"

"Something that may be relevant to Steven Auden's state of mind. He was seeing a counselor, someone I think you know."

Frederic's face stiffened. "You're not working for anybody's mother. You're looking for dirt. Who hired you?"

"Trust me," I said.

"I don't," he said.

I took out one of Ira's cards and slapped it down on the table. He looked at it without touching it. "So?"

"Tell me about Dísir," I said.

Frederic shot to his feet. "We're finished here."

"Hold on."

"You said it was my call. I'm calling it."

I'd come too far to have him just walk away. So I aimed for where it would hurt him most. "So you're the coward."

"What did you say?"

"Looking at your blog, you pose as somebody who's not afraid to take on anyone or anything. But maybe that's just because you can't handle anyone face-to-face."

"I can handle you," he said.

"Then sit down. And know that anything you tell me is in confidence, okay?"

He thought about it, then sat.

"I don't care what went on between you two," I said. "I want to know if you think she could have manipulated Steven Auden."

"To do what?" he said. "This?" He put a finger gun to his head and bent his thumb.

"To do anything."

"You think she manipulated me?" Frederic said.

"I have no idea," I said.

He sneered. "I manipulated her."

"Okay."

"Is she capable of playing mind games?" he said. "That's all she does, with that Viking BS."

"Is she why you left Roethke?" I said.

He shook his head. "I was gonna leave anyway." He smiled. "She was just a going away present."

"A sordid view," I said.

"According to who?"

"Ah yes, existentialism. You can't appeal to any moral authority."

"That's life," he said.

"You better hope so," I said.

"What's that mean?"

"You think this life is all there is?" I said.

"Of course," he said.

"Pretty stupid bet."

"Says who?"

"Pascal," I said.

"Who?"

"Listen, chum, if you're going to be Mr. Big Time Atheist, you'll have to go toe-to-toe with Pascal."

"Whatever."

"Did you know Steven Auden at all?"

"He looked like a wimp," Frederic said. "I don't associate with wimps."

"You must be the life of every party," I said.

"Your two minutes are up."

I shrugged, started to get up.

"Wait," he said. "Let me ask you a question."

"Sure."

"You really think there's a God?"

"Have you read the *Summa Theologica*?"

"No."

"You've got to spend some time in the cage. You've got to wrestle with the best if you're going to claim to be some great skeptic."

He leaned forward, chin jutting out. "How 'bout I wrestle with you right now?"

"I'd love to," I said, standing. "But I have business."

"Maybe another time," Frederic said. "Think you can take me?"

"You remind me of a guy I used to know," I said. "A boxer. His nickname was Ace-in-the-Hole."

"Because he always won?"

"Because he always ended up face down."

Frederic's cheeks got pink.

As I got up, I noticed the old man at the other table smiling at me. At least the colloquy had provided some entertainment.

With half the day shot, and nothing to show for it, I headed to FosterSynergisms. About halfway there I got a call from Destiny Jacobs.

"Something you should know," she said. "I'm at Bean There, I was just sitting here, when this big jerk comes over to me and says, 'You ought to learn to keep your mouth shut, or somebody'll shut it for you.' "

"What did this guy look like?" I said.

"He was big. Curly hair. Big bump on his nose."

"Just to be clear," I said, "this guy wasn't bald with a goatee?"

"No way," Destiny said.

"Did you say anything to him?"

"I told him I'd call the cops."

"What did he say?"

"He laughed, and said, 'Have fun proving what I said.' Then he left. He must have seen us talking."

"Or maybe someone told him."

"Wait, what? Do you think I'm I being watched?"

"You're a connection to Steven," I said. "Maybe Steven was onto something, that project you mentioned, and they think you know something about it."

"But I don't know what that project was."

"It could have been about lithium," I said. "Do you remember him saying anything about a company called Foster-Synergisms?"

"No."

"Did he ever mention a name that might have been associated with an energy company?"

"Not that I recall," Destiny said.

"Okay, then—"

"Wait," she said. "He did mention a name. Rebecca."

"Who's she?"

"I don't know. She might have been another student at Roethke. All he said was, 'Rebecca knows.' "

"Knows what?"

"He didn't say."

"Anything else," I said.

"No."

"Okay. Sorry this happened."

"No worries," Destiny said. "I just hope you find out what's going on."

"Makes two of us," I said.

"If you ever run into the curly-headed guy, I hope you can teach him to keep his bumpy nose out of other peoples' business."

"I'll definitely have that conversation," I said.

I got to the FosterSynergisms site. The approach was on a dirt road bounded by desert flora. I saw patches of Prince's Plume, an optimistic desert bush of the mustard family.

I also saw the NO TRESPASSING sign. That's where I stopped, got out, and walked to the edge of the site. It was lots of pipe, serried rows of steel storage units, a couple of trailers, and a big dome of some kind covered with a skein of rigging. It looked like a flying saucer had crashed by the Salton Sea and now the aliens were trying to fix it up to go home again.

There were two, huge pot-bellied furnaces belching thick, gray smoke into the air.

A guy came out of one of the trailers. He wore a yellow hardhat and waved at me.

"Can't be here, guy," he said.

"How you doing?" I said.

"You gotta go."

"Can I just ask you a question?" I said.

He frowned. "What about?"

"My name's Mike." I extended my hand.

He shook it. "Dwayne Emerson."

"This is all about batteries, right?" I said. "No more gas powered vehicles in California in fifteen years and all that?"

"Exactly," Emerson said.

Joey Feint used to say that men love to talk about their work. "Get them yakking about their profession and you're halfway to a confession," he once told me. "Get them gabbing about their trade and you've almost got it made."

So with all the sincerity I could muster, I said, "Is that really possible?"

Emerson nodded. "There's enough lithium in that bed for all the United States' future demand. And up to forty percent of the world's."

"I imagine there's some good old capitalist competition going on."

"Berkshire Hathaway operates ten geothermal power plants. EnergySource and Controlled Thermal Resources are also developing geothermal-lithium facilities. General Motors has already committed to source lithium from Controlled Thermal."

"How are you guys doing?"

"We're leading the charge. We'll be able to pump ten thousand gallons of brine per minute. And we use the steam from that brine to generate clean energy."

"Let me ask you this," I said. "You have any trouble with environmentalists?"

"Are you a reporter?" he said.

"Just an interested citizen."

"Well, I gotta ask you to leave, okay?"

"Are you the boss onsite?"

"You'll get the same answer from him," he said.

"I'll level with you, Mr. Emerson. I work for a lawyer up in L.A. I'm just gathering information on the whole enterprise down here, how things are done, what opposition you may have run into."

"Why?"

Over his shoulder I saw a Jeep approaching. Emerson looked.

"You wanted the boss?" he said. "You got him."

The Jeep pulled up. A stocky man with neatly combed gray hair hopped out. He wore jeans, cowboy boots and a denim shirt with the sleeves rolled halfway up his arms. If this was the boss, he was the hands-on type, not the sit-in-the-office-with-clean-fingernails type.

"What's going on here?" he said.

Emerson said, "Not sure, Mr. Foster."

"Frank Foster?" I said.

"Who are you?" Foster said.

"My name's Mike." I put out my hand.

Foster ignored it. "You can't read signs?"

I said, "Like I told your man here, I'm just trying to understand our electric future."

"Well go do some reading," Foster said.

"Any chance you could show me around?" I said.

"You a reporter?" Foster said.

"No," I said.

"In that case, you're trespassing," Foster said.

"Okay, I'm a reporter," I said.

"He works for a lawyer," Emerson said.

"Just a couple of questions," I said.

"You can talk to our legal counsel," Emerson said.

"Who might they be?" I said.

"Find out for yourself," Foster said. "But not around here. Dwayne, escort him out."

Foster hopped back in the Jeep and drove away.

"I guess that means I leave," I said.

"It does," Emerson said. "Where's your car?"

"Out at the No Trespassing sign," I said.

"Which is there for a reason," Emerson said.

I didn't move. A moment later the unmistakable sound of a Harley split the air. The rider was a side of beef in a black shirt. No helmet.

He stopped five feet from me and said to Emerson, "I'll take it from here."

I knew him. Bald, goatee. The guy from Jank's bar. He had a Taser in a holster on his belt and a nose that had seen better times.

"Isn't this a coincidence?" I said.

"Let's go," he said.

"Let's?" I said.

He smiled. "You walk. I follow."

"No thanks," I said.

"No choice. I'm gonna make sure you're gone."

"That could mean a couple of things," I said. "Why don't you come along with us, Mr. Emerson?"

Emerson gave me a dirty look. Then walked away.

"Goodbye, Mr. Emerson," I said.

"Don't come back," Emerson said.

After a beat, Goatee said, "Move."

"Let me ask you a question," I said. "You work with a guy your size with curly hair and a bump on his nose?"

Goatee put his hand on his weapon.

"You gonna tase me, bro?" I said.

"If you don't move," he said.

I didn't move.

He drew the Taser.

Synapses fired in my brain. I kicked the Taser out of his hand, and gave him a roundhouse foot to the face.

He toppled off the bike.

Goatee scampered to his feet and took a ready stance. He had a smirk on his face, as if this was the moment he'd been waiting for.

I didn't want this to drag on. Reinforcements could be on the way. The fastest way to a knockout is a hook to the jaw joint, just below the ear. But a skilled fighter knows how to protect against that.

So was Goatee a skilled fighter? Or one of the barroom boys who flings around fists of fury hoping to land something, anything?

Jimmy Sarducci, who knows the "sweet science" better than anyone I know, always says to watch the feet. A skilled boxer knows that a good punch starts from the ground, travels up through the hips, and finishes with shoulder rotation. The fist is just the finishing touch.

Goatee's feet were parallel, not a fighter's stance. And he was wind-milling his fists. Amateur hour.

I started wind-milling my fists at chest level. This was a fake out. I wanted him thinking I was on his level.

In reality, I had my hands curled into cement mode—fingers curled over the pads, thumb over the first and middle fingers, not stretched over the third. That rounds a fist instead of keeping it flat. It's a good way to break small bones.

Now I needed him to throw a punch. But he went into the

waiting game.

So I gave him the most basic of schoolyard tactics. I stuck my tongue out.

That did it. He charged, leading with a right cross aimed at my nose.

I leaned back, pulled my head. His punch came up short.

That left his right side open. I sent a left hook to his jaw, landing it with a satisfying crack. Just like a baseball player hitting a fastball off the fat part of the bat, sending the ball over the center field fence.

Goatee wobbled. His eyes rolled. His hands dropped.

I gave him another punch to the same spot. And down he went like a crate dropped from a longshoreman's pulley.

I got on the bike, started it, and rode out.

When I got to Spinoza I hopped off the bike and let it roll into a patch of Prince's Plume. I jumped in my car and drove off in a cloud of dust, Old West style.

I drove back to Morland. It was a little past 3:30 when I got to Roethke. I had a question for Nicholas Susa.

This time, there was a young man doing reception duty. He wasn't reading a book like Tomeka had been. He was double-thumbing his phone in rapid-fire, gamer style. He didn't look at me as he said, "Hold on."

He had glasses and some fuzz trying to be a beard. He wore a hot pink baseball hat with black birds all over it—an Edgar Allen Poe fever dream.

"Ahh!" he said, tossed the phone on the desk and looked up. " 'Sup?"

"Does that mean 'Can I help you?' " I said.

"Huh? Oh, yeah, sure."

"Is Dr. Susa available?" I said.

"Oh, um, maybe. What about?"

"He knows me," I said. "My name's Romeo."

"Romeo?"

"Need me to write it down for you?"

"Um, no." He looked at the landline on the desk. He stroked the fluff under his chin.

"I think you lift the handset first," I said.

"What? Oh. I'm just filling in." He took up the handset and held it like an early hominid examining a bone.

"Now you press a number," I said.

"I don't know which one," he said.

"Maybe it's written down somewhere."

"Yeah, but where?"

"How about we just knock on his door?"

"Yeah, um, I think that'll be all right." He got up, snatched his phone off the desk, and motioned for me to follow. We went through the side door and into a corridor. Gamer pointed to the first door on the left.

"Maybe I better knock," he said.

"You're doing a fine job," I said.

He went to the door and gave it a gentle rap. Susa's voice said, "Come in." My guide opened the door, stuck his head in and said, "There's a Romeo here who wants to see you."

No verbal response. A moment later Nicolas Susa came the door. He had a napkin in his shirt as if getting ready to eat barbecue.

"Mr. Romeo," he said.

"Can I have a minute?" I said.

"Sure, come in."

I stepped past Gamer, who looked relieved as Susa closed the door.

"Have a seat," Susa said.

I did. Susa sat at this desk, on which was a standing mirror and a makeup kit.

"I'm getting ready to do a Zoom interview with the PBS

station in Memphis," Susa said. "You mind if I touch up while we talk?"

"No problem," I said.

"I'm on a panel. How to deal with extreme crises." He dipped a makeup sponge in some flesh coloring and dabbed it under his eyes. Looking at the mirror, he said, "How is the investigation going?"

"I've talked to a few people," I said. "Professor Finney, for one."

"You talked to Roland?"

"I did."

"Wonderful man," Susa said.

"He said some nice things about you, too."

"What did you want to see me about?"

"I was wondering if there's a student here named Rebecca who might have been friends with Steven."

"Rebecca..." Susa paused, put the sponge down, opened a drawer and took out a tablet. "I think we only have one student with that name. Let me do a search." He tapped the tablet a few times. After a moment, he said, "Yes, Rebecca Seaton."

"Would it be all right if I spoke to her?"

He put the tablet on the desk. "Is that really necessary?"

I said, "What if I told you that pursuing justice is how I follow my bliss?"

Susa smiled. "I would say you are a man after my own heart. All right, I'll text her. But please, can you make it short and to the point?"

"I so pledge," I said.

Susa sent the text.

He removed the napkin from his shirt and crumpled it, tossed it in a wastebasket next to his desk.

"You're an interesting man," Susa said. "What would you think about visiting my class sometime, to speak?"

"I'm not much for public speaking," I said.

"Would you consider having a colloquy, then?

"My colloquies tend to make others colicky," I said. "I fear you'll be inundated with requests for safe spaces."

"I think you're being coy, Mr. Romeo. I think you delight in philosophical debate."

"Only when I'm off the clock," I said.

Susa touched one of the otters on his desktop water feature. I forgot which one it was. "If you don't mind my asking," he said, "how did you get into this line of work?"

"Fell into it, as they say."

"Any training involved?" he said.

"Just on the job," I said.

He nodded. "You look like someone who can handle himself in, you know, tough situations."

"I'd rather grow petunias," I said.

He laughed.

"I mean it," I said. "I love gardening, flowers. All flora, really."

Susa touched the other otter. "Now you are more than interesting. You're intriguing."

"I'm pretty simple," I said.

"I don't believe that," Susa said with a smile. He looked contemplatively at his otters, then said, "Would you consider being part of a book I'm writing?"

His phone cheeped. He looked at a text.

"She's coming to the office," Susa said.

"I appreciate it," I said.

"Now, about the book." Susa said. "It's going to be a popular treatment of what I teach, with interviews from interesting people. I'd like you to be one of them."

"I'm more the low profile type," I said.

"Well, it didn't hurt to ask." He told me a bit more about the book. He had an agent shopping the proposal. The agent was urging him to start on TikTok for promotion. I wondered what Socrates would have done on TikTok. But I think if he saw what was actually on it he'd call for the hemlock, stat.

A knock on the door. Susa said, "Come in."

A slight young woman with long, brown hair parted in the middle entered. She looked nervously between Susa and me.

"It's all right, Rebecca," Susa said. "This is Mr. Romeo. Mike, this is Rebecca Seaton."

"Hi," I said, standing to shake her hand. It was a small, delicate hand.

Susa said, "He works for a lawyer who is representing Steven Auden's mother. They are just trying to understand why Steven would want to kill himself."

"I feel so bad about that," Rebecca Seaton said. "He was so nice."

"Have a seat," Susa said. "Mr. Romeo just has a couple of questions."

She sat in the other chair, stiffly. I resumed my seat.

"How well did you know Steven?" I said.

"Not real well," Rebecca said. "He wasn't, like, a friend. But he was always nice when I, like, talked to him."

"What would you talk about?"

She shrugged. "One time I forgot where a class was and I asked him, and he said come with him, he was going there. So we walked and talked and he asked me how I liked Roethke and —" she gave Susa a quick glance—"I said I like it a lot."

"What did he say?"

"Nothing much. We got to the class."

"Any other times you can remember?"

She shifted in her chair. "Can I, like...can I know why are you asking me these questions?"

"Steven had an acquaintance named Rebecca," I said. "He

mentioned that she might know or remember something important. We thought that might be you."

Frowning as if to recall something and not finding it, she
said, "I don't see how."

"Did it ever seem to you that he was troubled about
something?"

"Um, no."

"Did he ever confide anything to you?"

"No," she said.

"Did he ever talk about environmental issues with you?"

"No."

"Are you friends with anyone who was close to Steven?"

She shook her head. "Sorry."

"All right," I said. "Thanks for coming in."

"Is that all, Dr. Susa?" she said.

"Yes, Rebecca," Susa said.

She stood and started out, stopped, turned around. "I hope
you can bring some kind of comfort to his mother. He was really
nice."

"Thanks," I said.

"K." She walked out of the office.

"Is there anything else I can do for you?" Susa said.

"I guess not," I said.

"I know this must be frustrating," Susa said. "But consider it
yin and yang."

"The yin I can see," I said. "It's the dang yang that's holding
me up."

Susa looked at his watch. "I need to get moving. Maybe
when this is all over, we can have a nice, long lunch."

E verything was pointing me back to square one. I hate
square one, especially when I've been wandering around
square six and seven, trying to find a move.

When I got to reception, Tomeka, the one I'd met before, was talking to the guy in the pink-and-black bird hat. It looked like she was showing him how the phone worked. As I walked by I gave her a wave, but said nothing.

Outside the desert sun was turning a late-afternoon red. It would soon be as gone as my prospects.

Instead of heading out, I went back to the dorms. Square one was Steven's room.

The door was open. A couple of guys were in there, sitting next to each other on the bed. One had dark hair and wore a loose sweatshirt that said *Roethke* on it. The other was dirty blond, wearing an unzipped camo jacket over a red T-shirt. They were looking at a book open between them. There were books and a laptop on the desk and a poster on the wall. The poster was of Albert Einstein sticking out his tongue.

The guy in the camo jacket looked at me.

"Are you that guy?" he said.

"What guy?" I said.

"The guy asking questions," he said. "About Steven."

"I'm that guy," I said. "Did you know him?"

"Not really."

"Is this your room now?"

"Yeah. I asked. I like the view. I can see the field from here."

The guy in the sweatshirt hadn't looked up from the book once.

"How about your friend here?" I asked.

"He doesn't go here," Camo said.

"I have no questions for him, then. Is the custodian around?"

"Eloi?" Camo said.

I nodded.

"I think he's in the bathroom," Camo said, and pointed. "That way."

"Thanks."

I walked to the unisex bathroom. The door was propped open with a yellow cone.

Inside, Eloi Kuprin pushed a mop near the sinks. He didn't see me.

"How you doing?" I said.

He whipped around like a scared rabbit.

"It's okay," I said. "Can I have a word with you?"

It was a full ten seconds before he said, "Why?"

"I'm just trying to cover all bases."

He looked like he didn't understand the phrase.

"Eloi...can I call you Eloi?"

He nodded.

"You've got nothing to worry about with me," I said.

"You scare me," he said.

"Why would that be?" I said.

"You're...big."

"I'm as gentle as a kitten," I said, not adding *when I want to be.*

Kuprin smiled. "I like kittens."

"And you liked Steven Auden, right?"

He nodded. "He was nice to me."

"Is everyone here nice to you?"

His brow furrowed. "Sometimes."

"Not always?"

He pulled his mop to his chest, like it would protect him. "Some people don't talk to me. It makes me feel bad."

"I know what that's like," I said.

"You do?"

"When I was in school, some people didn't talk to me. In fact...do you know what a swirly is?"

A little knowing smile broke out on his face. He nodded.

"I got some of those when I was a student," I said.

"That's not nice!"

"So maybe you can tell me if any other students here weren't nice to Steven."

He looked at the floor, trying to think. His eyes blinked and his head twitched a couple of times. Tourette syndrome? Oh, that'd be fine, me bringing on an episode.

"What are you doing?" a voice said.

Tomeka was at the bathroom door. Had she followed me?

"Just asking a question or two," I said.

"Can you please speak with me out here," Tomeka said.

I looked at Eloi Kuprin. There was a tear in his eye.

I went out.

Tomeka walked halfway down the hall, stopped, and said, "Please leave him alone. He was traumatized by all this."

"I understand," I said.

"Do you?"

"I think I do," I said.

"Can't you please be finished here? The students are starting to talk."

"What are they saying?" I said.

"It doesn't matter," she said. "We need to heal."

"Of course," I said. "I'm just trying to do my job."

"As are we all," she said. "I'll walk you to your car?"

"I'll find my own way," I said.

As I made for the exit I heard Eloi Kuprin's voice from down the hall.

"Steven was nice!"

A s I got in my car, Ira called.

"What on earth are you into up there?" he said.

"You're asking because?"

"The Imperial County Sheriff's office called me. There's an arrest warrant out for you. Assault. You want to tell me what happened?"

"Not over the phone."

"What's that supposed to mean?"

"I'm coming back," I said. "We need to talk this whole thing out."

"Let me come to you. We need to take care of the warrant. It's a cite-and-release. We'll get a date to appear before a judge."

"They can wait."

"Michael—"

"I need to breathe some L.A. air," I said.

"That's a first," Ira said.

"Too much stinks down here. You're going to help me clean it up."

"Michael, I strongly advise—"

"See you soon," I said, and clicked off.

I got back to the Best Value Motel around four. Troubadour Tim said he was sorry to see me go. He'd hoped I'd come to his Saturday performance in the park. I told him I'd put that in my bucket list. He seemed pleased.

"A girl came by to leave you something. Said her name was Destiny."

"She left me something?"

Troubadour Tim opened a drawer and pulled out rolled up paper with a rubber band around it.

"Looks like a scroll," T-Tim said, handing it to me. "She said to give her a call."

"Thanks," I said. "I'll do it on my way out."

"Out?"

"Heading back to L.A."

"Oh, that's too bad. I like talking to you."

"I may be back."

"Hope so! I can assure you we'll have a room for you."

"Why would I stay anywhere else?" I said.

. . .

Driving back to L.A., I knew my business in these parts was unfinished. And now I had the sheriff after me. I was on a wanted poster in Matt Dillon's office, like on the old *Gunsmoke* TV series. My dad loved watching those reruns. I'd watch with him as we discussed the mythos of the Old West. I remember once Matt Dillon had to arrest a friend who was suspected of murder. The friend swore he was innocent, and pleaded with Dillon to let him go. Dillon said no, he had to lock him up.

Dad said, "It's the code that counts."

"Morse Code?" I said. Even at ten years old I had a smart mouth on me.

"You can do better than that," Dad said. And then he went Socratic on me. "Does natural man tend toward good or evil?"

"Evil," I said.

"What constrains evil?"

"Force."

"Is force therefore good?"

"Not always," I said.

"When is it not good?"

"When the force is also evil."

"And when is force good?"

Mom walked in at that point with a big bowl of popcorn. She set it on the coffee table and smiled at Dad. She knew what was going on, winked at me, and left.

I grabbed a handful of popcorn.

"Answer before you eat," Dad said.

I thought about it. "Force is good when it conforms to law."

"All laws?"

"Just laws," I said.

"Are the laws Matt Dillon represents just laws?"

"I don't know," I said. "I haven't read them." Smart mouth.

"How about a law that says someone accused of murder must

be tried in court before a jury?"

"That would be just," I said.

"What about releasing the accused if you suspect he's innocent?"

"That's a tough one," I said.

"In the conflict between a just law and loyal friendship, which should prevail?"

I silently looked at the popcorn bowl.

"What choice is better for society?" Dad said.

"I guess the law," I said.

"Don't guess. Choose."

He had me. "Law."

"You may eat now," he said.

As I happily stuffed my face, Dad said, "Matt Dillon's code is to uphold a just law even though he doesn't want to. That's why, in this life, it's all about the code. A man's got to have one."

Dad ate some popcorn as we watched the rest of the show. Matt Dillon put his friend in jail, then figured out who the real killer was. He confronted the man, who drew his gun. Dillon outdrew him and shot him dead.

To me, that seemed like perfect justice all around.

I had the top down, soaking in some sun. I turned on the radio and found a news station.

In China, a protest over being locked down in Shanghai had been squelched by the police. The issue was COVID, vaccines that didn't work, and loss of personal autonomy. That sounded oddly familiar.

In L.A., the mayor was promising to do something about the homeless in words that sounded like the old mayor.

In Texas, a young man set the Guinness Book world record for ownership of video games. He had amassed 24,268 of them. Who says young people have nothing to live for these days?

A sports report was just beginning when I saw the motorcycle in my rear view. We were the only vehicles on this stretch of road, and he was closing fast. A big guy. I thought it might be Goatee, but the bike handle bars were set higher. He was fully helmeted, with a tinted facemask. Maybe it was Curly. One more biker and we'd have Three Stooges.

Maybe he was just a random guy. I dropped my speed so he could catch up and pass me if he wanted to.

He didn't want to. He kept about thirty yards behind me.

I sped up again. The bike stayed on my tail.

So what was the message? FosterSynergisms letting me know I was not welcome in these parts? Jank's Bar telling me they reserve the right to refuse service to anyone?

Maybe he wanted to talk. But he wasn't making any motion for me to pull over.

Or maybe he was a classic car lover and was admiring Spinoza from behind. I ruled that one out.

He began to get closer. When a Walmart truck came toward us from the opposite direction, he backed off again.

Once the truck was past, he started creeping up once more. He came around to my passenger side, matching my speed.

I looked at him.

The shaded visor looked at me.

His right hand pulled out a gun.

I slammed on the brakes.

He made a perfect bike spin—with gun in his hand, no less—and came at me from the front.

Which made me dead meat.

When a shrew, among the smallest of mammals, is cornered by a large predator, it will attack with everything it has.

All I had was Spinoza. I hit the gas. But bike guy anticipated the move and veered off to my right.

I gunned forward.

He did another spin and was back on me from the rear.

Dead meat again, with the back of my head as the target.

When I heard the first shot I instinctively lowered my head over the steering wheel.

The second shot sent Spinoza spinning across the opposite lane, doing a 180, and coming to rest on the soft sand of the shoulder.

I looked up and saw the bike heading back from whence it had come.

I got out and looked at my car. My right rear tire was shredded.

The message was loud and clear—don't come back.

Which made it a certainty I would.

I put the spare on Spinoza. A CHP officer stopped to check on me, set up a flare on the road while I worked. I didn't give him the cause. I'd just have to stay around and give statements and be prodded, and nothing would be done anyway. In twenty minutes I was back on the road.

It was dark when I got to Ira's. His house was filled with the warmth and smells of Ira's cooking.

"Got a brisket in the Dutch oven," Ira said. "With onions and potatoes."

"Let's eat."

We ate. As we did, I went over the last few days with him, up to and including the guy who shot out my tire. I must have looked like a prison escapee because Ira suggested I get a good night's sleep and we'd analyze in the morning. That sounded good to me.

He settled me in the guest room. Before I went to the land of Nod I called Sophie.

And said, "Home is the sailor, home from sea, and the hunter home from the hill."

"Longfellow?" Sophie said.

"Robert Louis Stevenson," I said.

"Meaning you're back?"

"Temporarily. I needed to touch base with Ira and figure out where we are. It was getting a little inhospitable down there."

"That phrase is loaded with hidden meaning," Sophie said.

"Loaded is apt," I said.

Silence.

I said, "How about I fill you in tomorrow, after your school day?"

"Perfect," Sophie said.

I could have used a little bit of perfect then. But as I began to drift off to sleep I remembered where the lines of the Stevenson poem came from. They're from a poem that begins, *Under the wide and starry sky, Dig the grave and let me lie.*

It's a poem about a grave marker.

Next morning, Friday, Ira had coffee brewing for me, bless him. My sleep hadn't been exactly restful. I kept seeing my name on a tombstone. At least no hand shot up from the grave, grabbing at my throat.

Ira had his usual tea. It was good to be in his presence.

"You look no worse for wear," Ira said.

"What does that even mean?" I said.

"You've had some wear, and you're looking better than expected."

"I'll take that."

"I'll cook you a nice breakfast, then we'll spend the morning figuring out where to go from here. How's that?"

"You're the boss," I said.

"I'll settle for friend," Ira said.

"That's a good settlement," I said. "Friends are in short supply these days."

"Too true," Ira said. "People are becoming more isolated, kids more addicted to screens. Time is no longer being invested in others, but in distractions. And with Artificial Intelligence directing it all."

"Science fiction catches up with reality," I said.

"Just a further manifestation of the activity of the great adversary."

"Meaning?"

"It's in the Book," Ira said. "And is there any other way to explain such extreme hate as we see around us? Such insanity and chaos? The old saying is that the idle brain is the devil's playground. Everything is geared toward idling people's brains. We don't teach kids how to think, but what to think. And when they grow up, we force them to think one way or we won't give them a job, or we'll take away the job they have. There is thus every incentive to turn off the brain, and it becomes a playground for the enemy of our souls."

"Cheery," I said.

"Ah, but to defeat the enemy it is first necessary to recognize his existence," Ira said.

"And then?"

"Shall not the judge of all the earth do right?"

"We'd better hope so," I said.

"Count on it," Ira said. "Why don't you get some sun while I cook?"

I poured myself another cup of coffee and took it to the bench in Ira's back yard, under the magnolia tree. The sun was unobscured and warmed my back. I closed my eyes and quieted my mind. Ralph, the little man, wasn't making any noise. He soon would be.

Twenty minutes later Ira called me in. He'd prepped scrambled eggs and lox, and toasted bagels, and a medley of fresh fruit. We kept the conversation light. At one point the subject turned to favorite movies. Ira chose *Sergeant York* starring Gary Cooper. "It's about real heroism," he said. "Not the kind that spouts the standard bull when accepting an Oscar."

When he asked about my favorite movie I had to give it some thought. When I was a kid, pudgy and clumsy, I wished I could be Tyrone Power in *The Mark of Zorro* or Errol Flynn in *The Adventures of Robin Hood.* But I kept coming back to that Western, *Shane,* starring Alan Ladd, about a mysterious gunfighter who rides into a violent valley one day. He's befriended by a settler and his family, and eventually defends them against a ruthless cattle man who has hired a gunman of his own. The gunman is played by Jack Palance.

Boom. "There's your enemy," I said. "Jack Palance is the devil. Shane is the deliverer. It's evil versus good."

"It always is," Ira said.

After breakfast I showered and shaved and joined Ira in the front room. He had set up his whiteboard on an easel.

"Some things to know," Ira said. "I found out from Mrs. Auden that Steven was ambidextrous. He wrote with his left hand, but threw with his right."

"Which pushes us back a square," I said.

"Perhaps. But it's not going to be as easy to convince the sheriff that we have a homicide."

"We need motive, means, and opportunity."

"Let's put it all on the board and see where we are." Ira took up a black marker. "Give me the names of the people you interviewed."

I read the names from my notes. Ira wrote them as a list on the left side of the board. Then he wrote the same names across the top, creating a grid. We started to make connections. Like in the box connecting Dísir and Frederic, Ira put a red X.

Some of the names had connections to other names. But at the bottom were two wild cards—Rebecca and the Motorcycle Guy who shot my tire out.

When the grid was all filled in, Ira and I looked at it in silence for a minute or two. Then Ira nodded, the way does when he makes a decision. "Let me do a little research on a couple of these names," he said. "I also want to do some digging in Steven's laptop. It was scrubbed of data, but as you know, there are ways."

"Are we getting any closer?" I said.

"Remember what Edison said after a thousand failed experiments—I now know a thousand ways that don't work."

"That and an infinite amount of time may prove very helpful," I said.

"Give me a little bit of time, then."

"For the stupendous breakfast, I grant it to you."

W hile Ira worked, I drove Spinoza to an auto-body shop in the Valley run by a former client of Ira's, Keith Johnson. Keith restored classic cars on the side, and was able to perform minor miracles on Spinoza once when my Mustang had been seriously shot up. He assured me the taillight could be done in a few hours.

So I Ubered over to Jimmy Sarducci's gym for a little workout. Jimmy, all five-feet-two of him (without lifts in his shoes) was watching a couple of fighters in the ring.

"Stick and move," he said. "Stick and move!"

"Hey, Jimmy."

"Mike!"

"Who've you got there?"

Jimmy looked at the fighters. "You'd think I was runnin' a Heinz warehouse here. I got nothin' but tomato cans."

Tomato can is boxing lingo for a pushover fighter. They're often used as an easy victory to advance a superior fighter. They are, in other words, kicked down the road like an empty tomato can.

"Still wish you'd put on the gloves for me," Jimmy said. "You still got it."

"Still got all my teeth, too," I said.

"Teeth can be replaced," Jimmy said. "Like wives." Jimmy's been married three times.

I worked out a couple of hours, showered, went back to Johnson's auto-body shop. I waited some, but in short order Spinoza was ready for the road again.

I t was a couple of hours before I'd meet up with Sophie, so I drove back to Ira's, taking the Valley route to the Hollywood Freeway. According to my research, and people like Jimmy who grew up here, the San Fernando Valley was once the quintessential post-war suburb, a verdant garden of the American dream, a flowering of the burgeoning middle class. Single-family homes bloomed on calm streets dotted with trees—palms, eucalyptus, pepper, orange. People sat outside with their neighbors on warm summer evenings. They walked around, even at night, frequenting mom-and-pop businesses on the main strips like Ventura and Sherman Way. The aerospace industry was booming. Jobs were plentiful. Crime was low. The birth rate was high.

But the years passed, as they are wont to do, and blight hit the garden. Aerospace started dying after the moon landing, and disappeared after the Cold War ended. Heavier government regulations sped the death.

Big retailers moved in, putting the heat on small businesses. The heartier ones hung on until the lockdown madness. Few survived that intact.

The homes I was passing had a hang-dog look. What were once lush lawns have given way to brown patches, weeds, and cracked cement. Paint has faded, walls have graffiti—oh, excuse me, "urban art."

There are holdouts, though, mostly oldsters keeping spruced-up the homes they've lived in for thirty or forty or fifty years. You can see them with their garden hoses and hedge clippers, clinging to the pursuit of happiness before it's choked to death by the oily hands of state and local bureaucrats.

Which is why you don't hear songs about the California dream anymore. No more "bowers of flowers" blooming in the Spring, as in Al Jolson's "California Here I Come," or the Beach Boys' wishing for more "California Girls," or Randy Newman gargling, "I Love L.A."

"California, Here I Go" would be more timely, but you probably couldn't dance to it.

I ra was at his computer when I came in. He waved at me to sit.
"Let me tell you about Frank Foster," he said. "Graduated from Michigan Technological University with a degree in environmental engineering. Got an MBA from Wharton. Went to work for an energy company called QRN in Detroit. Was in charge of the company's electric and natural gas distribution and regulatory compliance. Started FosterSynergisms ten years ago."

"Personal life?"

"Wife, Penny, and two kids, a son and daughter. The son—Ansel—died. Maybe suicide."

I perked up. "There's an interesting connection. Any details on that?"

"This was in Florida. His son owned a yacht," Ira said. "Went out and never came back. They found the boat on the open sea with nobody on it."

"Why do they think it was suicide?"

"Chain and anchor were missing."

"That sounds sketchy to me," I said. "Most men use a gun to end it."

"This is a curious data point to add to the mix."

"When was this?" I said.

"Seven years ago," Ira said.

I went to the whiteboard and added ANSEL to the list of names.

"Get ready for another curious point," Ira said. "Foster's daughter."

"Yes?"

"Her name is Becky."

I put an asterisk next to the name REBECCA on the whiteboard, then drew a line from the asterisk to FRANK FOSTER and put a question mark over the line.

"Any idea where we can find this Becky?" I said.

"Not yet," Ira said. "Assuming she is the mysterious Rebecca, what makes us think she'll say anything? She is Foster's daughter, after all."

"Find her for me," I said. "At this point we need to grab any straw that comes up."

"I am your humble servant," Ira said.

I drove over to The Constantine Academy and waited for Sophie. A line of cars drove through the gate, picking up kids. Education was humming along in Los Angeles. At least in this spot. In other places, not so much. Yesterday there'd been a double stabbing at a high school, multiple fentanyl overdoses at a middle school, and a traffic collision outside an elementary school that sent a kid to the hospital.

When Sophie came out she looked refreshed. Teaching does that for her.

We drove up to Mulholland and parked in a spot with a view

of the Valley. I asked Sophie how the kids were liking *Romeo and Juliet.*

"As expected," she said. "Some have taken to the story, some have worked through the language, but one..."

"Yes?"

She shook her head. "One of my girls asked, completely innocently, whether Romeo was a stalker."

"She used that word?"

"No doubt picked up from some celebrity on TV or TikTok," Sophie said. "What is the future of romantic love when kids think this way?"

"They don't have to think," I said. "The machine will pick their mates."

"Now there's a depressing thought. Let's change the subject."

"To what?"

"You."

"Deep subject," I said.

"Don't I know it," Sophie said. "You were going to fill me in?"

"I don't want to bore you."

"That's one thing you're incapable of," Sophie said. "Go ahead."

"Oh, not much to tell," I said. "A guy took a shot at me."

"What!"

"It was more of a warning shot. Took out one of my tires."

"At this point I should say something like 'Unbelievable." But with you, it's not. Do you have any idea who it was?"

"A guy on a motorcycle. Had a helmet on, I couldn't see his face. But I'm going to go find that face and make it talk."

Sophie looked at our entwined hands.

"Romeo's world," I said. "Is it how you pictured it?"

"It's how I know it is," she said.

"Change of subject again," I said. "Do you ever think about the Spartans?"

"Not my first choice of things to think about," she said. "I know about them raising boys to be warriors."

"What about the women?" I said.

"I believe Spartan girls trained like the boys in things like wrestling, boxing, and throwing the javelin."

"Why do you suppose they did that?"

"Well, if the men were off fighting, and some rogue Persians showed up, the women could punch them in the face or put a javelin through them. Anything to protect their children."

I made a pearl-clutching motion on my throat. "How violent!"

Sophie smiled. "I see where you are going with this."

"I'm going somewhere?"

"We've talked about violence before. You know my history. And we both know it's kept us apart. Now you want to know if anything's changed."

"We can skip it if you'd like," I said.

"Oh no, not now," she said. "You've put it on the table."

"How do you think the Dodgers will do this year?"

"Quiet, Romeo. You want to know if I identify in any way with Spartan women, don't you?"

"Dodger pitching looks strong."

She put her finger on my lips. "I will tell you this. After two years of teaching kids, if anyone came on school grounds with evil intent, and I were armed, I would have no hesitation at all."

She removed her finger.

"I want to kiss you now," I said.

"Then you'd better do it," she said.

I did.

B y the time I got back to Paradise Cove, the night sky was up and blinking. When it's clear in L.A. you take it in while you can.

I went down to the beach. Venus was strutting her stuff among the stars. Below was a string of colored gems, the lights of Santa Monica. There would be people up and down the pier riding the Pacific Wheel and the West Coaster, or downing buckets of shrimp at Bubba Gump's, or bar bites at Rusty's Surf Ranch. Living normal lives, or as close you can get to that in Crazy Town.

Could I be among the normal? Could I give that to Sophie?

Sisyphus popped into my head. Condemned by Zeus to roll a boulder up a hill for all eternity, only to see it roll back down every time, Sisyphus would never know peace. No shrimp or bar bites or fun rides. Or a woman to love.

I raised my fist to the sky. "Bring it, Zeus," I said.

When lightning didn't strike, I walked back to my place and found someone waiting for me on the front porch.

"You're back!" C Dog said.

"You have wonderful powers of observation," I said.

"I saw your car," he said. "You got a beer?"

I went inside and got a couple of Coronas and came back to the porch.

"How's things with your girl?" I asked.

He shook his head. "I don't know. Why is it so messed up?"

"You ask an eternal question, my friend, about the vicissitudes of love."

"The whats?"

"The way things get mixed up without any warning."

"That's it!" C Dog said.

"You turn to the poets on this one, C. There is no happiness higher than love, or the other side of it, the pain."

"Yeah."

"The question is, is it worth it?" I paused for a sip. "You know the old saying? It is better to have loved and lost than never to have loved at all."

"What's it mean?"

"Only you can answer that," I said. "It was true for Romeo and Juliet, not so much for Samson and Delilah."

"I've heard of them," C Dog said. "In the Bible, right?"

"He was a warrior," I said. "She was a hair stylist. Things didn't work out."

C Dog sighed. "I want things to work out."

"That's a good sign," I said.

"So what should I do?"

"Think about a code," I said.

"Code?"

"Ever hear of the code of chivalry?"

He shook his head.

"It's a set of rules the knights of old signed onto, to keep them from acting like complete jerks."

"Is that what I am?"

"You might be, and not know it. The code keeps us in line. Men are born to be strong, but are also prone to jerkdom. The code points us the other way. It says things like use your strength to protect the weak and the children, don't slander people, keep your word, don't be a coward when it comes time to fight."

C Dog was silent for a moment, then said, "I can see that."

"And this," I said. "Love one woman only, cleave to her, and honor her with years of noble deeds."

"Whoa!"

"Don't hear that on TikTok, do you?" I said.

"What's that mean, cleave?" C Dog said.

"Do you love your guitar?"

"Of course!"

"When you play it, it's part of you, right?"

"Oh yeah."

"And if someone tried to take it, you'd fight to keep it."

"Nobody takes my axe."

"And you write songs for it."

"All the time."

"You honor your guitar," I said. "And cleave to it. And honor it with years of songs. Shouldn't you treat a woman as more than a guitar?"

He leaned back and took a pull on his beer.

"You got to help me figure this out," he said.

"We'll figure it out together," I said.

He held up his bottle and we clinked.

L ater, as I was settling down with *The Little Sister*, Ira called.

"There's someone you should see," he said. "I found her name in a message backup on Steven's laptop. Her name is Kari Innes. She's a journalist."

"They still exist?" I said.

"Not in the old-school sense," Ira said. "J schools turn out crusaders now, not reporters."

"So who is this crusader?"

"She has her own podcast. From what I gather, she likes breaking stories about celebs. Who is sleeping with whom. You know, important stuff."

"And I should see her why?"

"I called her. Interestingly, she's heard about you."

"How?" I said.

"It's what she does," Ira said. "That's how she put it, anyway. She says there's something you should know about Steven. And she wants to know what we know."

"That's all she said?"

"She doesn't like doing things over the phone," Ira said. "She wants a live meeting."

"Okay," I said. "When?"

"Tomorrow."

"Where?"

"Whittier."

"Why Whittier?"

"It's where she's based," Ira said. "She wants to meet you in public, at a place called Mimo's Cafe. Eleven o'clock."

"Shouldn't we be meeting in a dark, underground garage?"

"This is not a movie, dear boy."

"It should be," I said. "Cary Grant should play me."

"I believe Cary Grant is dead."

"What a comeback it would be," I said.

"One other item," Ira said. "I received a call from your friend Coltrane Smith. He wishes to speak to you."

Coltrane Smith was an LAPD detective who'd given me some help in the past.

"He say what about?" I asked.

"He did not," Ira said. "Which makes me wonder if there's something you're not telling me."

"But you always wonder that."

"Point taken."

"How about this?" I said. "When I find out what he wants, I'll fill you in."

"A red-letter day that will be."

"You don't have to rub it in," I said.

Whittier is one of the original suburbs of L.A., about twenty minutes east of downtown. It was named for the poet John Greenleaf Whittier, who school kids in L.A. have likely never heard of. There's a park with a statue of Whittier in the middle of it. Even though he was a strong abolitionist, his statue was marred back in the tear-them-down mob craze. Didn't matter who it was. If it was a statue, desecrate it. Join the fun.

Mimo's Café was on Greenleaf Street, also named for the poet. It had inside and outside seating. I scanned the umbrella tables outside and spotted a lone woman working on a laptop. She could have been a college student or funky dress designer.

She wore red-frame glasses, all the brighter set against the deep black of her hair, most of which was in a side ponytail draping over her shoulder. Her top was red and white stripes, like an old-time sailor, her pants black and her high top canvas sneakers red. A drink with a straw in it was on the table.

"Kari Innes?"

She looked up. "Mr. Romeo?"

"Mike will do," I said. "May I?"

"Please."

I pulled out the other chair and sat.

"I feel like I should ask for a password," I said.

"What?"

"This is all a little cloak-and-dagger, isn't it?"

"You mean meeting here?" she said.

"That's what I mean," I said.

"I need to be in control of the interviews I do," she said, giving me a look that said *Don't crowd me.*

"It was a long drive out here," I said. "I hope it's not for nothing."

"We'll see about that," she said. She picked up her drink. "You want something to drink? Eat? They make great sammies."

"No, thanks. Let's talk."

"Fair enough," she said. "What do you know about me?"

"You have a podcast that does local muckraking."

"Muck what?"

"The muckrakers were journalists of the progressive era, dishing dirt on big business and political corruption. You're sort of in that tradition, I gather."

"I'm writing that down," she said, and tapped her keyboard.

I said, "As Mr. Rosen told you, we represent the mother of Steven Auden. We know he contacted you. I'd like to know what that was all about."

"Hold up there," Kari Innes said. "If we're going to get

anywhere it'll need to be give and take. I want to know everything you know about Steven."

"Then we have a problem," I said. "Client confidentiality."

She leaned back in her chair, folding her arms across her chest. "Then maybe this whole thing was for nothing after all."

Hardball. No wonder she wanted me to drive all the way out here. It was her leverage.

"I'm not interested in dancing," I said. "How about we each show a card, and see where we are?"

"You first," she said.

"Only if this is off the record," I said.

"Really?"

"Really."

"I don't think so," she said.

"Fine," I said. "Have nice day."

I got up.

"Okay," she said. "Off the record."

I sat. "Steven was reportedly upset about the environment. You spend a lot of your time on that issue. Steven had some sort of connection with FosterSynergisms."

"Go on," she said.

"Your turn to show a card."

She tapped her finger on the table. Which card to play? She said, "Steven contacted me and told me he had a big story I might be interested in."

"This was out of the blue?"

"Completely," Kari Innes said.

"How did he contact you?"

"I have a contact page on my website. I get a lot of trolls and haters, but I also get usable content this way. We arranged a meeting."

"And?"

"Your turn to show a card."

"I went out to FosterSynergisms a couple of days ago," I

said. "Frank Foster was there. He told me to get lost and one of his security guys tried to make that happen."

Her eyes lit up. "Was there a fight?"

"Not much of one," I said.

She smiled. "Now this is getting interesting. Let me use this. I'll keep you anonymous."

"Still off the record," I said. "But I do have a hole card, an ace. I'm not going to play it yet. But you'll be interested when I do."

"What if you're bluffing?" she said.

"Do I look like some slick, dishonest card sharp?" I said.

"I don't know you well enough to say."

"I'll take that as a yes. But you're a reporter and that at least makes you curious. Every now and then you have to go out on a limb, right? Like Nellie Bly."

"Who?"

"One of the first investigative reporters," I said. "In the 1880s she went undercover by posing as a patient in an insane asylum. Her reporting on the conditions for the *New York World* led to reforms. All I'm asking is for you to trust me on this one point."

She thought about it. "All right," she said. "Steven wanted to know if I could help him find someone named Albert Staley."

"Did he tell you why?"

She shook her head. "He said he couldn't tell me yet. I got frustrated at that point and told him not to talk to me again until he had something worth publishing."

"How'd he take that?"

"Not like I expected," she said. "I thought he'd sulk. He looked like the sulky type."

"What does the sulky type look like?"

"Not like you."

"I can get a good sulk on if I put my mind to it," I said.

"You have somebody who can pull you out of it?" she said.

"That's a pretty direct question."

"I'm a journalist, remember?"

"Okay, then. Still off the record?"

"Sure."

"I do have someone who can pull me out," I said.

"Love interest?" she said.

"Let's get back on the subject."

Her eyes danced. She was enjoying this.

"All right," she said. "I was about to say that Steven got a determined look in his eyes, and said he would get back to me very soon, and that I would definitely be interested in what he had to say."

"Did he ever get back to you?"

"No," she said. "Next thing I know he committed suicide."

"You have a theory on why?" I said.

"He left a note," she said. "Concern over climate change. Thought the world was coming to an end. He wanted to rest. I can see that. Things are pretty messed up."

"So other than this Albert Staley, did he mention any other names to you?"

"No."

"Rebecca, maybe?"

"Who's that?" she said.

"I don't know," I said. "Just another name we came across."

"Is that your hole card?" she said.

I shook my head.

"Well then?" she said.

"I owe it to you," I said. "But I have a condition."

She frowned.

I said, "I want you to hold onto this, don't broadcast anything, until I get more evidence. In return, I promise you'll get the whole thing, exclusive. Does that interest you?"

"You've got my attention," she said.

"Here it is then," I said. "I have reason to believe Steven Auden did not kill himself."

Her eyes widened. "You serious?"

"I wouldn't be here if I wasn't," I said.

"What are your reasons?" she said.

"That'll be part of the story I give you."

"How long might that take?"

"I don't know," I said. "I don't even know if I'll get any more evidence. Right now it's thin. If you had what I have, an editor would tell you not to run the story."

"Great, just great," she said.

"Good things come to those who wait," I said.

"Yeah? Who said that?"

"It was either Abraham Lincoln or some guy at a bus stop," I said. "So be patient."

"I'm no good at waiting," she said. "Things move too fast."

"Which is why so much garbage is spewed."

"Excuse me?"

"Axe grinders who fancy themselves journalists jump on some event, twist it into a story that fits their narrative, and send it out with clickbait headlines to beat the competition. But when the facts blow up in their faces, after some innocent life has been destroyed, they clam up, blow it off, and go salivating for their next victim."

Her mouth dropped open.

"Disagree?" I said.

"Well, yeah."

"Why?"

"I just do," she said.

"That's not an answer," I said.

"It's good enough for me."

"Let me put it to you this way," I said. "Would you rather be first or be right?"

"Can't I be both?" she said.

"If you had to choose one."

She thought about it, but didn't answer.

I said, "It used to be a reporter would come in with a scoop, and the editor would ask what the evidence was. If it was thin, he'd say go out and get more evidence. See, they used to have the idea that truth mattered in reporting. But that was a long time ago."

"It still matters," she said.

"Then answer my question. Would you rather be first or be right?"

"Of course I want to be right," she said.

"Which is why we wait," I said.

W hat a surprise that I hit a traffic snag on the way back to Ira's. I crawled my way along the 101 through downtown. That gave me time to take in the graffiti on the overpass walls and freeway signs. The City of Angels was turning into the jungle of taggers. Downtown used to be a place to relax over chop suey at Grand Central Market, or with a stroll along Olvera Street, or a browse in The Last Bookstore. Now it's all you can do to avoid the hypes and the homeless, the dopers and the dealers, the naked and the dead. Maxim Gorky would have had a field day here gathering characters for a musical version of *The Lower Depths*.

I ra was in his wheelchair, reading, when I came in.

"You look pale and wan," Ira said.

"And a good day to you," I said.

"What, you want I should lie? You want I should tell you that you are the picture of health and vitality?"

"Yeah," I said. "Then feed me."

"That would not be the truth, and would not be beneficial to you," Ira said. "The Mishnah permits a little white lie only to keep someone from gratuitous pain. There is a curious instance in the book of Genesis, when three angels drop by Abraham's tent. They have a message for Abe, who is old, nearly one hundred."

"I'll bet he looked pale and wan," I said.

"One of the angels informs Abraham that his wife Sarah, no spring chicken herself, is going to bear him a son. Sarah is in another tent and overhears this. And she laughs and says to herself, basically, how can this be when I'm withered and my husband is too old to...you get the picture. Their tent has ceased to be a pleasure dome."

"Oh my," I said.

"Here is the curious part. The angel knows she said it, and says to Abraham, 'Why did Sarah laugh, and say, shall I bear a child, old as I am?' "

I waited. Ira, in rabbinic fashion, let me wait. Finally I put my hands out. "And?"

"Notice what the angel left out." Ira said, a gleam in his eye. "He left out that part about Abraham being too old to, ahem, fulfill his husbandly duty. Why did the angel withhold that? Because if Abraham heard that, he would feel his wife disrespected him. God was not about to break up this couple. Thus, to spare someone's feelings from being deeply and gratuitously hurt, it is permitted to tell a white lie. I judged your feelings would not be gratuitously hurt if I told you the truth, that you looked pale and wan. So I went ahead and told you. On the flip side, telling you that you look terrific would not do either of us any good. Especially you. And that is how ethics is done, my boy."

"That was quite a journey over a trivial remark," I said.

"But worth the trip," Ira said.

"And now that the journey has ended, what's for lunch?"

"There's kreplach from Canter's in the kitchen," Ira said. "Still warm."

I went into the kitchen, got a bowl, and poured what was left of the kreplach into it. I took it back to the living room-slash-office and sat on the window bench.

"I trust this will perk me right up," I said. "So I don't look so pale."

"And wan," Ira said.

"What else can you tell me?" I spooned a dumpling into my mouth.

Ira wheeled over to his desk and computer.

"Becky Foster," he said. "I believe I found her."

"Where?"

"She runs a little antique shop in San Luis Obispo called Junk Sisters. I found a news story about it, and they dropped that she was the daughter of Frank Foster."

"That's a long drive," I said.

"What else have you got going on?" Ira said.

"I was going to work on my tan."

"Drive with the top down."

"Your wisdom knows no bounds," I said. "How about a little wisdom on what to say to her?"

"You should tell her you have a mutual friend, then mention Steven's name. See if her face twitches."

"And if it does?"

"See how much resistance she gives you," Ira said. "That will tell us where to put some pressure."

"While I'm gone you can do a little more work," I said. "Another name to locate. Albert Staley. Kari Innes gave it to me. It came from Steven."

"Context?" Ira said.

"None," I said.

"How helpful. It would be easier if his name was Pudge Heffelfinger."

"Agreed," I said.

"When will you head to San Luis Obispo?" Ira asked.

"I will follow the Macbeth advice," I said. "Tomorrow, and tomorrow, and tomorrow."

"Isn't that speech about the futility of life? Out, out, brief candle and all that?"

"Life's but a walking shadow," I said. "A poor player that struts and frets his hour upon the stage, and then is heard no more. It is a tale told by an idiot, full of sound and fury, signifying nothing."

"I'm glad you don't believe that."

"Don't I?"

"There's too much good in you," Ira said. "And kreplach, too. There is meaning in both those things. This is why Jews especially enjoy kreplach on Purim. The Jews were saved when the evil Haman was defeated. The meat hidden within the dough represents God's mercy, wrapped within his attribute of justice."

I drank the last of the broth from the bowl. "We'll see," I said.

A t eight the next morning I started for San Luis Obispo. I took PCH to Las Virgenes, then cut over to the 101 for the three-hour drive north. I called Coltrane Smith and left him a message. When I was cruising past Ventura he called back.

"Need me to buy tickets to the Policeman's Ball?" I said.

"What is this, 1945?" Coltrane Smith said. Buying tickets to the Policeman's Ball is slang for a bribe. Or was in Raymond Chandler's day.

"Anything to keep the cops off my back," I said.

"Funny you should say that."

"Oh?"

"I was scrolling the day sheets when something interesting caught my eye. Seems there was an incident in the Valley. A woman called it in, said a big guy in a Hawaiian shirt beat the ever-loving out of a guy in a truck, then left him battered on the side of the street and drove off in a green convertible."

"What is the city coming to?" I said.

"And I'm just taking a flyer here, but I wondered if you might know anything about it."

"Let me think. Was the guy in the Hawaiian shirt described as ruggedly handsome?"

"Not that I recall."

"Then I have no idea who it could have been."

"Oh, you have some idea. Want to tell me more?"

"Do I need to consult my lawyer?"

"I'm not the investigating officer," Smith said. "But I may be able to offer advice to a friend."

"Short version, then," I said. "That guy in the truck followed me off the freeway, intent on doing me harm. He had a baseball bat and took out one of my taillights. He wanted to take out my head. You know me. Things kind of went south from there. Anyway, he lost the fight and I drove away."

"So you're saying it was some kind of self defense?"

"My kind," I said.

Pause.

Smith said, "I'll see what I can do. Meanwhile, don't get into any more trouble."

"I'm afraid that ship has sailed," I said.

"I'll pretend I didn't hear that," Smith said.

North of Santa Barbara the 101 cut inland, taking me through a canyon and pouring me out into unspoiled portions of California. It reminded me why so many people want to live here. Or used to. Recent rains had the hills blanketed with green. Seems whenever the Grand Poobahs in charge of the state announce another severe, man-made drought, Mother Nature slaps their knuckles with a steady downpour. Of course, the Poobahs don't do anything to preserve the surplus life-giving water, eagerly awaiting the moment they can shout about man-made-drought once more and limit water usage again. How they love to limit everything, except the size of government.

D owntown SLO had an abundance of trees, especially ficus, that gave it a quaint, rural feel. But the shirtless, bearded man screaming at the passing cars gave a feel of a different sort, like a splotch of Los Angeles or San Francisco had been added just to keep people on edge.

I found the shop called Junk Sisters on Broad Street. I parked at a meter and went in.

It was more organized than a true junk store, more eclectic, with high-end antiques. On the right were several racks of shirts and coats, and a shelf of old shoes. On the left, tables of vintage items—a record player, a couple of toasters, a set of five mugs with Hopalong Cassidy on them. A wall displayed guitars and ukuleles and a couple of trumpets. And this was just the front portion of the store, which seemed to go on forever. Several customers were poking around.

In the middle of it all was a station with a cash register. A young woman in a Cal Poly sweatshirt worked the register, ringing up a sale to an older woman.

I went over and stood behind the customer. When she cleared out, Cal Poly looked at me, waiting for me to place something on the counter.

"Is Rebecca around?" I said.

The girl frowned. "I don't know of any...wait, do you mean Becky?"

"Yes."

"She's in the back. Did you want to see her about something?"

"Yes," I said. "We have a mutual friend."

"Oh, okay. Let me go see." She left her post and went toward the back of the store, and through a curtained door.

I flipped through a spinner display of plastic necklaces.

A minute later a woman came out, followed by the college girl. The woman was short and round, maybe forty. Her forearms were sleeved with tats. One of her ears was studded with enough metal to interrupt a radio signal.

She gave me an up-and-down look as she approached. "You wanted to see me?"

"Rebecca?" I said.

"Becky," she said. "Who are you?"

"My name's Mike. I drove up from L.A."

"Why?"

"I think we have a mutual friend."

"Who?"

"Steven Auden."

Pause. "I'm afraid I don't know who that is. You drove all this way to ask me that?"

"I like to drive," I said.

"I guess so," she said. "Anything else?"

"Maybe he knew you," I said. "In some other way."

"Knew?"

"He's dead."

She frowned. It looked like genuine confusion.

"Why are you telling me this?" Becky said.

"Steven knew someone named Rebecca," I said.

"I don't call myself that, okay? I haven't since I was in high school. So I'm not this person, okay? I don't think there's any more to say."

"I talked to your father," I said.

"No, you didn't."

"Frank Foster isn't your father?"

Her eyes went cold. "Get out of here."

"Now wait—"

"How much is he paying you?"

"He's not—"

"Get out!"

Someone came through the curtain. Looked like a woman, tall, with broad shoulders.

"What's going on?" this person said, in a deep, throaty voice.

"Nothing," Becky said. "This guy was just leaving."

The tall one gave me a look that stuck halfway out my back.

"You want me to get Mario?" Tall said.

"Can I explain?" I said to Becky. "It's not what you think."

"I'll get Mario," Tall said, and went back through the curtain.

"Mario?" I said.

"You don't want to meet Mario," Becky said.

"Give me five minutes," I said.

"I don't see why I should give you any minutes."

I took a chance. The way she'd said she didn't use the name Rebecca anymore, and her reaction to mention of her father, told me I was dealing with estrangement here. Maybe I could position myself on her side.

I said, "Your father had one of his punks try to throw me off his lithium mining site."

She looked at me a moment. The beginning of a smile came to her face.

At which point Tall returned, this time with a definite male. He was a little bigger than me, with the build of a prison enforcer. He wasted no time getting in my face.

"You're leaving," he said.

"It's okay, Mario," Becky said.

"What?" Mario said.

"I can handle this," Becky said.

Mario looked disappointed. "Don't make no trouble," he said

to me.

"Not me," I said.

"Come with me," Becky said. I followed her, feeling the other four eyeballs bore into my back. We went through the curtain. The room was packed with random junk, old paper-backs, clothes, shoes. Becky went through an open door with a sign that said OFFICE.

One look at the room and I thought a better sentiment would be ABANDON HOPE, ALL YE WHO ENTER HERE. To describe it as a mess would be to insult most messes. There was a desk hidden under mounds of papers and trinkets and wadded up clothes. There was a chair behind the desk. Becky sat in it. She rubbed her face, then said, "So you were at the site?"

"I was," I said.

"And you actually talked to Frank?"

"You call him Frank?"

She waved her hand in the air, as if swatting a fly. "We don't have a relationship."

"I'm sorry to hear that," I said.

"Why?"

"Parents and children shouldn't be estranged."

"What world are you living in?"

"I like to think about what should be," I said.

"What good does that do?" she said.

"It beats drugs."

"You sure?"

I let that one go.

"So tell me why you were there," she said. "And then tell my why you're here."

I looked around for a chair. There wasn't any.

"Sit on those boxes," Becky said, nodding toward a stack of three against the wall.

I sat on them. They must have been packed. There was no give in them.

"I work for a lawyer in L.A.," I said. "We represent the mother of Steven Auden. He was a student at a place called the Roethke Spiritual Center in Morland. He's dead. Maybe suicide. Maybe not. We're trying to figure it out."

"And what does dear old Frank Foster have to do with it?" Becky picked up a vape pen from her desk and inhaled.

I said, "Steven was working on a project that may have had something to do with the environment, and FosterSynergisms."

She blew mist into the air. It smelled like blueberries and cheesecake. "Doesn't surprise me. How much do you know about my father?"

"Only a little. Wharton MBA. Starts an energy company. American success story."

"If by success you mean doing whatever it takes to whoever stands in the way, then yeah."

"You would say ruthless?"

She snorted. "That would be a mild way of putting it. When my mom was dying of cancer, he started an affair. I was in high school. When I confronted him about it he kicked me out of the house. Kicked me out! I went to the cops and they did jack. I went to a lawyer, and when she found out it was my father with his team of fancy legal eagles, she wouldn't take the case. Should I go on?"

"You don't have to," I said.

"So mom dies. There's nothing to keep me around, so off I went into the world. Which stinks, by the way."

"What about Ansel?" I said.

Her face got hard. "What do you know about him?"

"He had his troubles," I said. "Didn't he commit suicide?"

"Or got iced."

"Murdered?"

She shrugged. "He ran around with some very sleazy people. He was into things. Drugs. I don't even like to think about it. We were close when we were kids. But he changed. See what a lovely family life I have? And why'd you have to come here, anyway?"

She took a hit from the vape pen. There was pain in her eyes.

"Sorry to dredge all this up," I said.

She exhaled. "Look, If you want to know if my father is capable of having somebody killed, I'd say yes. He's screwed up, and he passed that gene on to me. I've been fighting it for twenty years. Stay away from him. That's my advice to you."

"I don't think I can take that advice," I said.

"That's too bad," she said.

I left the store and went to my car. And found Mario leaning on the hood, his feet on the curb.

"You were lucky," he said.

"Fantastic," I said.

"Yeah, lucky."

"Did I win something?" I said. "A cheese grater, maybe?"

"Just don't come back," he said. He stood up and faced me. "Got it?"

"You're not helping tourism," I said.

His answer was to spit on Spinoza's hood.

"Really?" I said.

He spat a second one.

"Mario, what good is that?" I said. "You want to live in a world where people treat each other this way?"

He started to walk away.

"Ho, there," I said. "You forgot something."

He turned around.

"You need to wipe it off," I said.

He smiled and didn't move.

"Let me put it this way," I said. "I'd appreciate it if you'd wipe your saliva off my hood."

He was a statue.

I said, "It would be better if this could be done without more persuasion."

He made a come-to-me gesture with his hands.

"Now, see that?" I said. "You're one of these guys who just doesn't have a good day unless he beats somebody up. Is that the kind of life you want to live?"

He was at the end of his intellectual capacity and gave me a two-word sendoff. He started walking away again.

I ran and grabbed his shirt collar. A hard pull had him falling backward, with my leg out. He tripped over it and hit the ground. A hammer punch to the side of his head rang his bell. His eyes rolled up.

I ripped off a section of his shirt.

I took the remnant to my car and wiped off Mario's spit.

And heard a boy's voice. "Wow!"

He was ten feet away from Mario, holding a skateboard. Maybe twelve years old.

Mario was still on his back, blinking.

I approached. The boy backed up, eyeing me.

I stuffed the rag in the pocket of what was left of Mario's shirt.

I looked at the boy. "Stay in school and don't do drugs," I said.

Then I got in Spinoza and got out of town.

I got hungry around Paso Robles, but kept on driving. I made it all the way down to Ventura, a beach town about an hour north of Los Angeles. I got off the freeway and started cruising for a place to get something to eat. I pulled into a place advertising fish tacos. It looked popular enough. There was a line at the ordering window.

When it was my turn I ordered two of their tempura fish tacos and an 805, a blond ale brewed in California. I took my order to an outside table. If Diogenes had been searching for an honest fish taco he would've stopped here. They were good and filling and started to return me to a semblance of order, if not peace.

I drove down to Oxnard and cut over to Pacific Coast Highway. The sun was setting by the time I got to Zuma Beach. It was a big, red ball dropping into the sea. I pulled over and watched it go down. It cut through a couple of dark clouds as it went.

Ten minutes later I was in Paradise Cove.

I tossed my duffel in the corner and lay down on the futon. I closed my eyes and listened to the ocean. Next thing I knew I woke up to the sound of, "Hey, man!"

C Dog was at the screen door.

"Come on in," I said.

As he did, I flicked on a light.

"Were you asleep?" C Dog said.

"Just dozing," I said. "I've been on the road."

"You here to stay?"

"I doubt it."

"I wanted to tell you something."

"Go ahead."

He sat on the sofa. "Things aren't looking so good between Dakota and me."

"Oh?"

"We kinda broke up," he said.

"You broke up with her?"

"Well, she kinda broke up with me."

"How do you feel about that?" I said.

"It sucks."

"C, you once told me you felt like she was crowding you."

"Yeah."

"Then why does it suck she broke up with you?"

"I don't know! It's that thing, I mean things of love you told me about."

"Things?"

"Vicious tudes or something like that."

"Vicissitudes," I said. "But your way is actually a good way to put it."

C Dog rubbed his hair with his fingers, as if trying to remove sand. "What should I do?"

"Let me ask you," I said. "Are you upset because it's a blow to your ego? Or because you've lost something that feels like a part of yourself?"

"Man, I don't know!"

"You're not alone, pal," I said. "Many a man has had a hard time knowing what to do about love." I almost snorted at the irony of me being the one to say that.

"You've got to have confidence and strength. But you have to be confident without being a blowhard."

"What's a blowhard?"

"A braggart."

"What's a braggart?"

"A loudmouth about how great he is."

"Okay. I get that."

"Let your confidence be a quiet confidence," I said. "Part of that is not caring what other people think of you, except the ones you are close to and trust."

"I trust you, man."

"Then there's strength. It's not just physical strength, but strength of will and character. Grace under pressure. A guy who gets easily stressed out in the face of challenges is not attractive. Though you won't hear this in college anymore, a woman's biology is part of the equation."

"Whoa, slow down. What's that mean?"

"It's instinct. A woman gives birth and wants a man who can protect her offspring. This is denied by many, but it's like denying gravity. Jump off a roof and you're still going to go down."

"That's a lot of stuff to think about."

"It takes a lot of stuff to be a man," I said. "Add a sense of humor and being kind to most people."

"Most?"

"You don't have to be kind to jerks. But to children and waiters and mothers and the woman you're with, yes."

"Where did you come up with all this?" C Dog said.

"I didn't," I said. "This has been worked out over thousands of years, by philosophers and poets, and through long experience. It's called wisdom, which is in short supply these days. That's why I have you reading good books. Speaking of which, you're due for a new one."

"I guess," he said.

"You want to be on your own now? I can certainly—"

"No, man! Lay it on me."

"I'd love to give you *Romeo and Juliet*, but I don't know if you're ready for Shakespeare."

C Dog pursed his lips, thought about it. "Let's do it," he said.

I nodded. "Now that's a manly thing to do, accept a challenge. I'll get you a copy."

"No," he said. "I'll buy it myself."

"That's the ticket!" I said. "That's putting skin in the game. Good move."

C Dog smiled. That was reward enough for one night.

I n the morning I went for my swim and ate breakfast listening to Gershwin. Around nine I headed for Ira's.

On the way I called Sophie. It went to voicemail. Of course. It was Monday morning and she was teaching. So I left a message that ended with, "Remind me to tell you about vicious tudes."

Ira had fresh bagels and roasted garlic schmear waiting for me. And coffee.

As we ate, I gave him my report on San Luis Obispo, which added up to—

"It was all a big schmear of nothing," I said.

"I approve of the Yiddish," Ira said. "Though the proper word here would be bupkis. As in zip, zero, nada."

"Well, that's what we've got."

"Only for the time being. Justice will prevail. This is the message of God."

"Tell him to hurry up," I said.

"Joseph had to wait years in prison," Ira said. "But God was with him. And what man meant for evil God meant for good."

"It's a fine story," I said.

"It's fine history, and it makes me content," Ira said.

"Contentment would be nice. Where can I buy some?"

"It's free," Ira said. "If you know where to look for it."

"The Book?"

"Start with the Proverbs. You know, the Proverbs are directed to young men."

"Oh?"

" 'My son, hear the instruction of your father.' And do you know why?"

"I have a feeling you're going to tell me," I said.

"Because the largest class of stupid idiots is young men. Thus, they are the ones who most need the restraint of wisdom. And the fear of the Lord is the beginning of wisdom. And, I might add, justice. Your pal Spinoza would agree."

"Oh?"

"He and Hobbes. Man in a state of pure nature has no concept of justice. It's might makes right. What else is there?"

"The law of club and fang," I said.

"Jack London," Ira said. "A secularist."

"But he loved dogs," I said.

"Dogs have an innate sense of justice. What was it Justice

Holmes said? Even a dog knows the difference between being tripped over and being kicked."

"Right now there's a whole lot of kicking going on," I said.

"Point proved," Ira said.

"I've got some kicking left to do, too."

"As long as your foot is just."

"My foot is asleep," I said, shaking my right leg.

"As long as your mind isn't, dear boy. Shall we pursue justice?"

"Let's."

"I've got a lead for you," Ira said. He wheeled his chair to his computer. He tapped the keyboard. "The name Albert Staley."

"Yes?"

A record of some sort appeared on the screen. Ira said, "I did an extensive search of properties sold in and around El Centro. It took some time, but I found the sale of a home. Seller, Albert Staley."

"When was this?"

"Two years ago."

"Any idea where he is now?"

"Not yet."

"Terrific," I said. "I'm not interested in driving all over the state, if he's even in the state anymore."

"I don't expect you to," Ira said. "Just south."

"Back to the belly of the beast?"

"You might try the house and see if anyone there knows where he might have moved."

"Can I rest for a day?" I said.

"*Mi casa es su casa*," Ira said.

"You can't say that."

"Why not?"

"Cultural appropriation," I said.

"Get out of my house," Ira said.

I did get out. Went for a walk. I usually stroll past where the

Argo Bookstore used to be. It was where I met Sophie once upon a time. Back when there were still local businesses operating without fear of flash mobs and prosecutors who did not prosecute. Instead of deterrence, the laws unenforced act as an incentive to criminals. Which makes you want to grab the D.A. by the lapels and shout "Wake up!" But then you'd get arrested as a domestic terrorist and tossed in the clink. You'd be better off shoplifting.

Now the Argo space was closed up. A faded *For Lease* sign was on the window, the same one I'd seen last time I walked by the place.

In just a few months this section of Los Angeles, like every other section, looked worse off. The combination of feckless politicians, vagrant drug addicts, and the lingering effects of the toxic lockdown era was tanking the City of Angels. Once a place where people came to dream, it was turning into a nightmare that jittered citizens into renting moving vans or investing in home security and handguns.

But the weather's nice.

Back at Ira's I finished *The Little Sister*, then took a nap. A little after three-thirty, Sophie called me.

"I'm at Ira's," I said.

"Are you here to stay?"

"I'm going back to Morland tomorrow."

"Again?"

"I've got to go where the leads are," I said.

"This is your life," she said.

"Maybe I should open a nursery," I said.

"For kids?"

"For flowers," I said. "Nice, quiet existence."

She laughed. "I'm trying to picture that for you, but the picture is fuzzy."

"Everything about this case is fuzzy."

"Tell me more," Sophie said.

"I'm starting to believe Steven's death was a hit. Planned out. By someone who knew what they were doing. I have a couple of candidates, guys on motorcycles."

"Biker gang?"

"No, these guys are employees. They work for somebody. At least one of them works for Frank Foster. There's a connection there. Foster is the head of a firm mining for lithium. But it just seems too pat, too easy."

"What does?"

"That Foster would have put out a contract on Steven Auden. He has lawyers. They're more effective than assassins. We're also trying find a mystery woman named Rebecca."

"Hm, like the novel."

"And the Hitchcock movie," I said.

"With a twist," Sophie said. "Maybe that's what's going on for you."

"Meaning?"

"Maybe there's romantic intrigue," she said.

"You know," I said, "I'm half inclined to consider that. I've got nothing else."

"Mike?"

"Yes?"

"Be safe. Come back, and stay awhile."

"Done and done."

Now I knew what Sisyphus would be doing if he were around today. He'd be driving, always driving, up and down California, trying to get some place, and when he got there it wasn't the right place, and he'd have to drive again, and again, and again, world without end, amen.

He'd pass the same scenery, over and over. The big dinosaurs. The Salton Sea. And he'd smell the stench. He'd pull into the same motel and inside—

"Hey, you're back!" Troubadour Tim said.

"I'm back," I said.

"Fantastic. I got a new song to try out. Want to hear it?"

"Maybe later," I said. "What I want is a room and a place where I can park my car where it won't be seen."

He thought about it. "I can manage that. There's a space out back, an old car port. We could put a tarp over your car."

"That'll work," I said. "And I'll want to rent a car."

"Sure. There's a place in town. Not one of the bigs, but I know the guy, and he's pretty reliable when he's not drinking."

"How about you arrange a delivery?"

"I could..."

"But?"

He shrugged.

"Got ya," I said. I took a couple of twenties out of my wallet and put them on the counter. "Delivery fee."

He took the bills. "Sweet."

"Give me a room in the back," I said.

"You can pretty much have your pick," he said.

I pulled Spinoza around the back and found the old car port. Troubadour Tim met me there, carrying a tarp. We threw it over my car and secured it with rope.

The room had one benefit. It was slightly less smelly than the Bette Davis room. Things were looking up.

I did a hundred push-ups and a hundred crunches. I stayed on the floor and looked at the ceiling. I started to feel less like Sisyphus and more like Alfred Dreyfus on Devil's Island. How long was I fated to be in this place? Where was my vindication, my escape?

Twenty minutes went by. Then Tim called the room and told me to come to the office.

There was a man with him, white bearded, dressed in jeans

and denim shirt.

"Got you a car," Tim said. "This is Hal Crockett."

"Howdy," the bearded man said. "Come out and see."

I followed him through the front doors, Tim tagging along.

A dingy, reddish sedan was parked in front.

I did a double take. "Isuzu?" I said. "How many million miles on this thing?"

Hal puffed out his chest. "This thing, as you put it, has a lot of life left in her. She runs like a dream."

"I just don't want to wake up with a dead car under me," I said.

"This is my business, okay? I don't rent out junk, okay?"

"He doesn't mean anything, Hal," Troubadour Tim said.

"He sounds like he means something," Hal said.

"I mean it's a deal," I said.

We went back inside and I signed the papers. Hal ran my credit card through a reader attached to his phone. Then he asked Tim to drop him off back at his shop.

I got in the sedan and started it up. I pulled out of the lot and headed for Highway 86. The car did not run like a dream. It rumbled like a fevered reverie.

But it did move.

T he address Ira had given me was in a rundown section of El Centro. It was a smallish house, yellow with blue trim. I walked to the door. The sweet-skunky smell of baking marijuana was in the air. I couldn't tell where it came from.

I knocked. A moment later a woman's voice said, "Yes?"

"Hello," I said in my Mr. Rogers tone. "Didn't Albert Staley used to live here?"

Pause. Then, "Um, I don't know."

"I'm an old friend. I'm trying to locate him."

Silence.

I said, "May I ask if there's anyone here who might know where he relocated?"

"I can't help you."

"Maybe if I left you my card..."

No response.

"Hello?" I said.

No response.

So I tried the house next door, and found the source of the Mary Jane.

T here were three of them, guys in their early twenties, sitting in an open garage. They sat on lawn chairs. One of them, a guy with a pinched face and buzz cut, held a weed pipe and a Bic lighter. A car with an open hood took up half the space.

They looked at me unconcerned, but by no means friendly.

"Hi, fellas," I said.

No response.

"Maybe you can help me out," I said.

No help was offered. The buzz cut guy fired up the bowl of hippie lettuce with the Bic.

I said, "I wonder if any of you knew the guy who used to live next door, name of Albert Staley."

Six red-rimmed eyes exchanged glances. Three heads shook.

"Couple babes live there," Buzz Cut said.

All three smiled. The scrawniest one made a grunting sound. Sounded like the monkey house at the zoo.

I said, "Anybody in the neighborhood who might know?"

Buzz Cut said, "Maybe the old guy."

"Yeah," Scrawny said. "The old guy."

"He's not a babe, though," Buzz cut said. The trio broke into laughter.

"Where can I find this old guy?" I said.

Buzz Cut passed the pipe to Scrawny. "Across the street, red house," he said. "But watch your nuts."

"Excuse me?" I said.

"He tried to kick me in the nuts once," Buzz Cut said.

For some reason this brought another round of laughter.

"Well, you all have fun now," I said.

"It's what we do," Buzz Cut said, and cackled.

F eeling like a pinball, I went across the street. The red house looked like it could use a lot of work. The front lawn, if you could call it that, was ankle-deep weeds. I knocked on the door. No answer. Knocked again. Nothing.

Then I heard a *putt putt* engine sound, getting louder. A few seconds later a man riding a lawn tractor came around the side of the house. He was gaunt and gray and holding a three-pronged lawn hoe in one hand. He looked like a latter-day Quixote with horse and lance. He spotted me and came at me, head on. Maybe he thought I was a windmill.

When he got within five feet he cut the engine.

"Who are you?" he said. His voice had gravel in it. He was probably in his late seventies.

"Name's Mike," I said. "I—"

"You here for the septic?"

"No, I—"

"Then what good are you? I don't want what you're sellin'."

"Not selling anything."

"What do you want?"

"Just to ask a question. I'm looking for Albert Staley."

"Who?"

"Used to live across the street, in the yellow house."

He squinted at the house. "Oh yeah. Him. Why?"

"It's a professional matter," I said.

"You a cop?"

"Now why would you ask that, Mr..."

"You're talking around yourself," he said. "I can't help you."

"Or won't."

He shrugged. "I got work to do."

"Look, I'll level with you," I said. I took out Ira's card, held it out for him. "Albert Staley may have some information helpful to a case I'm working on. That's all. I'd just like to ask him a couple of questions. Whoever's living there now didn't seem to want to help."

"Renters," the man said. "They wouldn't know anything."

"Can you help me out?"

"I don't know. People want to keep private, they should be left alone."

"Is that what Albert Staley wanted?"

"I don't know. I didn't know him all that much. He was divorced, bought the house, was in there a few years, then sold and went away."

"Any idea why?"

"I didn't ask."

"Never talked to him?"

"I didn't say that. He walked his dog. Sometimes he'd walk by here and I'd see him and he'd say something like 'Good morning' and I'd grunt."

"Grunt?"

"I don't see anything good about morning. Just means you got a whole day to deal with."

"Not exactly a cheery view of life," I said.

"Got news for you," he said. "Life ain't cheery. Even if you got a dog. He tried to smile at me."

"Tried?"

"It didn't seem real," he said. "Like those weirdos at that college."

I perked up. "Roethke?"

"Crazy name."

"Was Albert Staley connected with it?"

"No idea," he said. "I'm just sayin' he...what's that smell?"

"Maybe a skunk," I said. "Did he—"

"Ain't a skunk. It's those punks across the street!" He lasered his look at the open garage.

I said, "Look, Mr...can I know your name?"

"No," he said, and handed me back the card. "And I don't need this. Unless you can help me get rid of those punks."

"That's not my business," I said.

"Then what good are you?"

"That's the second time you've said that."

"Then get the message," he said. "And get gone."

W hat a friendly town. I knocked on a few more doors in the neighborhood. Same result. The one person who opened the door, an older woman, knew about the man who walked his dog, but nothing else.

The way many of the houses looked—not well kept—indicated to me these were mostly rental properties. The days of close-knit neighborhoods where people knew each other and lived in the same place for years were a relic of the past, like those dinosaurs I kept passing on the freeway.

I drove on. There's a park in El Centro with a man-made pond and some ducks. I parked. The ducks were swimming around like they didn't realize they were trapped in El Centro.

Like I was.

I called Roethke. A familiar voice answered.

"Tomeka?" I said.

"Who is this?" she said.

"Mike Romeo."

"Oh. Hello." On the chilly side.

I said, "I was wondering if you could help me out. I'm trying to track down a name. I wanted to know if this name has any association with Roethke. Albert Staley. Ring a bell?"

Pause. "Um, no."

"Maybe I could ask Dr. Susa."

"He's not in today. Can I give him a message?"

"Sure," I said. "If you can get it to him right away."

"What is the message?"

I gave her Staley's name and spelled it for her. Then I hung up and watched the ducks for a while. They were happily swimming around, oblivious to the ways of the world. Brought to mind when I swim in the ocean. For those minutes I'm also oblivious, or at least happily forgetful. I don't feel hate or rage or despair. I don't feel like I have to punch a wall or somebody's face. The water is my refuge, the waves are my ramparts.

A couple of kids went down to the edge of the pond and threw bread crumbs out to the ducks. They swam over and quacked for more.

Dr. Susa called me back.

"You were interested in a name," he said. "An Alan Staley?"

"Albert," I said.

"Right. Don't know an Albert Staley. Should I?"

"I just gave it a shot."

"Your investigation continues?" he said.

"Such as it is," I said.

"Is there anything else I can do for you?"

"I guess not."

"You don't sound sure."

"If I think of anything, I'll call you."

"Please do."

I thanked him and cut the call.

The ducks swam around the pond. Then a hawk came swooping down over the water. The ducks scattered. The bird of prey did a loop in the air and came back the other way.

The kids who'd been feeding the ducks screamed and waved

their arms. The hawk seemed to laugh, looped again, and made one more pass.

It was clear to me then. I couldn't keep swimming around. If something was going to happen, I'd have to make it happen. I'd have to be the hawk. I'd have to find some ducks, and do some swooping.

I drove back to Morland and parked across the street from Jank's Bar.

It took two hours before the big mallard arrived.

He parked his motorcycle at the curb, took off his tinted helmet and ran his hand through his thatch of curls. He put the helmet over the mirror and went inside.

I gave him five minutes, then walked across the street and went in.

He was sitting at the bar talking to Tommy, the screenwriting bartender. There were two geezers at one end of the bar, nursing beers.

Tommy's eyes went wide as I sat on the stool next to Curly.

"Howdy," I said.

Curly looked at me. His face registered four or five iterations of what the—? He didn't say anything. The pronounced bump on his nose seemed to be turning red, like his own personal alarm system.

Tommy just stood there.

"You going to serve me?" I said.

Tommy said nothing.

"A Coke," I said. "No ice."

Curly recovered his tongue and said, "What do you want?"

"Conversation," I said.

"Not with me," he said.

"Business talk, then," I said.

"I got no business with you," Curly said.

Tommy put a glass of Coke in front of me. Then left us.

"But you owe me money," I said. "For my tire."

"Don't know what you're talkin' about," Curly said, in a casual way that indicated he knew exactly what I was talking about.

"I'll settle for a hundred and fifty bucks," I said.

"Move along."

"But first, tell me why Frank Foster hired you to shoot up my car."

Curly smiled and shook his head. "I don't know what your deal is, but you are out there, man."

"I know all about you, *man*. I know about what you try to do to people to get them to clam up. I can ID your helmet and your bike. I can do a lot of things, including giving you another knob on your sniffer. All you have to do is tell me why Frank Foster sent you after me, and I'm willing to forget about the tire."

He picked up his glass of beer and looked at it. "Whyn't you get out of here while you can still walk?"

"Tommy!" I said. The bartender came over, concern on his face.

I said, "This guy just said I should get out of here, while I can still walk. Did you write that line? Because it's pretty lame and you'll never make it as a screenwriter with that stuff."

The move I'd been waiting for finally came. I figured it would be a back-handed arm sweep at my face. But Curly tried to deliver a roundhouse left by turning forty-five degrees on his stool.

I leaned back. The punch went wide. I gave him a right to the jaw. That, and his momentum, sent him off the stool and onto the floor.

One of the geezers shouted, "Whoa!"

Tommy said, "Take that outside!"

Curly was quicker than I thought. He rolled and got to his

feet and grabbed his stool in one smooth motion. He wasted no time in swinging the stool at my head.

Instinct propelled me forward, ducking, so the stool hit my back. My shoulder hit Curly in the ribs, driving him a few steps backward.

"Stop it!" Tommy said.

Curly charged me. I stepped to the side and pulled his shirt, sending him over my leg, sprawling.

This time I didn't let him get up. A heel stomp to the head dazed him. I took a fat wallet out of his back pocket. There were three twenties, a five, and a couple of ones in it. I took them and put them in my pocket.

I looked at his driver's license. His name was Wiley Gant. He was as ugly in his photo as he was in life, just a little younger.

A high-pitched voice shouted, "Don't move!"

I turned toward the door. A guy in a police uniform had a gun on me. He was in a triangle stance, ready to fire.

"Hands on top of your head!"

I complied.

A short, round policewoman came in, hand on her holstered sidearm.

"Cuff him," the tall officer said to her.

She responded immediately, with a don't-mess-with me look plastered to her face.

"Arms behind you," she said to me.

I dropped the wallet on Wiley Gant's prone body.

"This is the guy you should arrest," I said. "He attacked me."

"Hands behind you," the tall officer said, keeping the gun at the ready.

I let the little cop put the bracelets on me.

The tall cop lowered his weapon, but kept both hands on it.

"Outside," he said.

"Let's go," said the woman.

"What about him?" I said with a nod toward Gant.

"Now," Tall Cop said.

A police car was at the curb.

"Morland Police?" I said.

"That's right," Tall said.

"So the legends are true," I said.

The short one opened the backseat door and said, "Get in."

"Don't you think you're rushing things here?" I said.

"Get in," Tall said.

"What about the guy who attacked me?"

"You wanna resist?" Tall said.

"I want a chance to explain."

"You'll get your chance," Tall said. "Get in."

I got in.

So did the cops, quick. A grill separated back from front. Tall drove, and burned rubber.

"How did you guys happen to be there?" I said.

"Be quiet," Tall said.

"Why aren't you interested in the truth?" I said. "Somebody give you orders to take me?"

Silence.

"If you're intending to rub me out," I said, "I'd like to know about it."

That brought a snort from Short.

"Tell him," she said to Tall.

"Not yet," he said.

He turned onto a strip of road that took us out to the desert darkness. About half a mile and he pulled off the road onto the shoulder and cut the engine. It was a perfect spot for a murder.

Tall turned and spoke to me through the grate. "Listen up. We know who you are. We saw you cross the street and go into Jank's. You know the sheriff has an arrest warrant out for you?"

"I'm aware," I said. "You taking me in?"

"Heck no," Tall said, then looked at his partner. "Give the man his hands."

Short got out of the car. She came around and opened the back seat door and took some keys off her belt.

"Turn and slide toward me, please," she said.

I turned and slid. She unlocked the cuffs, got out and closed the door. She slipped back into her seat next to the driver. The odor of the Salton Sea seeped into the car.

"You've got my attention," I said.

"We had to get you out of there. You know who you were fighting with?"

"Wiley Gant," I said.

"A real thug," Tall said. "With punk friends. It could have gone bad for you."

"Why should you care?"

"You've been sniffing around FosterSynergisms," Tall said.

"You know this how?" I said.

"Police work," Tall said.

"Why is the Morland Police Department interested in Foster Synergisms?" I said.

"Only a third of the department."

"You and your partner," I said.

"That's it," Tall said.

"You're going rogue on this?"

"I wouldn't say that," Tall said. "This office needs a detective division."

"Which I'm looking at now," I said.

"Just the start," Tall said. "You and I may have common interests."

"Frank Foster?"

"He's good," Small said to her partner. I think she was referring to me.

"There's something local Foster's into, and it's criminal."

"Any idea what that is?"

"I was hoping you might have some insight on that. What brought you down here?"

"This is all very nice," I said. "Only before I tell you what I know, how do I know you're not working for Foster?"

"What?"

"Corrupt local cops," I said. "It's been known to happen."

"He's got a point," Short said.

"We're not working for Foster," Tall said. "I don't know how to prove it to you, though."

"Start with your names," I said.

"All right," Tall said. "I'm Mal Peters, this is Lana Reed. We both grew up here. We could get you character references, but it's a little late right now."

"Morland seems like a town you'd want to get out of as soon as you were able," I said. "What made you stay?"

"We didn't," Peters said. "We came back. I actually got halfway onto the Los Angeles Police Department, but when I saw the way cops doing their jobs got dragged before review boards, it didn't seem like a rosy future. My dad told me there was an opening here, and I took it."

"And I went to San Diego State," Lana Reed said. "I dropped out to take care of my mom. I needed a job, and saw in the post office they were expanding the police department."

"From four to six," Peters said.

"I was the first woman," Reed said.

"Trailblazer," Peters said. "We hit it off."

"What got you interested in Foster?" I said.

"We picked up a guy at Jank's on a drunk and disorderly," Peters said. "We were taking him in to cool off. He thought he was going to get arrested and started crying in the car, saying things, like Foster was a liar and a killer, and was into something really bad. He said he wanted to tell us, but not from jail. I figured he was just blowing smoke, but after we let him go the next day, he said he wanted to meet with us, and he'd contact us. He never did."

"Where is he now?" I said.

"Don't know," Peters said. "He disappeared. That's when we started to get interested in Foster."

"Real interested," Reed said.

"What did you do about it?" I said.

"Started watching, listening. In a small town, you can do that."

"Like Yogi Berra said," I said.

"Who?" Reed said.

"You don't know about Yogi Berra?"

She shook her head.

"What do they teach at San Diego State?" I said.

"Beats me," Reed said, and smiled.

"Yogi Berra was a famous baseball player, catcher for the New York Yankees. Known for his philosophical insights. Such as, 'You can observe a lot just by watching.' "

"That's for sure," Reed said.

Peters said, "About a year and a half ago, somebody bought an old house on the edge of town, a place that had been abandoned for years. An old lady moved in."

"An elderly woman," Reed said.

Peters frowned. "Like I said, an old lady moved it. She's kept pretty much to herself ever since. Don't know why, but that makes me curious."

"Curiosity, well placed, is a good trait in a detective," I said. "I used to work for one when I was younger."

"So I got to cruising by the house on my rounds. Only once saw her outside. I stopped. I was going to say hello and welcome her to Morland, but she saw me and went back inside."

"Now *I'm* curious," I said.

"Just wait," Peters said. "A week or so later I went by and saw a motorcycle parked in the driveway."

"Curiouser," I said.

"I didn't know what to think about that. There's a detached garage that maybe's being used as a dwelling. I drove half a mile past, there's a place you can still see the house. I watched for awhile and a guy came out and got on the bike and took off."

"Let me guess," I said. "Wiley Gant."

"I couldn't tell. Too far away. So I bought some binoculars, for next time."

"Was there a next time?"

"Oh yeah," Peters said. "The next time there was a sweet red Porsche parked outside. I did the same thing, drove to the spot, and used the glasses. Eventually a guy came out, middle-aged guy, good shape. I didn't know him. But I had jotted down the license plate."

"Good detective work," I said.

"First chance I got, I went to the office and ran it. Got the registration. You want to guess who owns it?"

"Frank Foster," I said.

"This guy is good," Reed said.

"I try," I said.

Peters said, "I'd like to talk to the lady, but I can't just go up and question her. If I did that, she'd probably call Cap and I'd be out on my can."

"Your captain," I said.

"Strict," Peters said. "Then we heard about you. You seem to get into it with the thugs."

"I have a way about me," I said.

"So here we are," Peters said. "Does that satisfy you?"

"Maybe eighty percent," I said. "But at this point I'm willing to take a chance. Tell me, does the name Steven Auden mean anything to you?"

The officers looked at each other. Then Peters said, "No. Should it?"

"He was a student at Roethke," I said.

"Wait a second," Peters said. "The kid who shot himself?"

"That's the one," I said.

"What about him?"

"He was working on something," I said. "May have had to do with Foster, the environment, I don't know what all else. But he dropped a name, Rebecca, and it turns out Foster has a daughter by that name, only she goes by Becky, and doesn't have any love for her old man. I tracked her down in San Luis Obispo. She warned me to be careful."

"She was right," Peters said.

"But I don't think she's the Rebecca Steven referred to. You know anybody around here by that name?"

"I'm sure we could come up with a Rebecca or two, if we thought it was important," Peters said.

"How about the name Albert Staley?" I said.

"Doesn't ring a bell," Peters said.

"Could that mean Al Manly?" Reed said. "Works at the hardware store."

"Not the one," I said. "Which is the problem. Everything's a dead end. What if I had a chat with the old lady?"

"She does not seem the chatting type," Peters said.

"What if I search the place?"

"Excuse me?"

"Break in when she's not there," I said.

"You can't do that," Peters said.

"Why not?"

"It's against the law, for one thing."

"That doesn't matter these days, or haven't you noticed? You can burn down a city and not even get a ticket."

"He's right about that," Reed said.

"Suppose you found something," Peters said. "You can't use it."

"Use it for what?" I said.

"Well, in court."

"I'm not interested in court," I said. "What I want is information. The Fourth Amendment doesn't apply, because I'm a private citizen, not law enforcement."

"But we are," Peters said. "You can't be doing this because of us."

"I haven't heard you tell me to go in," I said. "You've warned me not to. Okay, I've been warned."

"That still leaves the problem of her being in the house. I don't know when she goes out. I've seen her in town buying groceries."

"We—I mean I—would have to watch the house."

"You really want to do that?"

"I've got nothing else to do," I said. "This place is one big cul-de-sac. I'm tired of going round and round and coming up with bupkis."

"Bupkis?" Reed said.

"A Yiddish word," I said. "It means zip, zero, nada."

"Understand this," Peters said. "If something goes wrong, we can't help you."

"Kind of the story of my life," I said.

Peters cleared his throat. He looked at Reed. She nodded. Then he gave me the address.

They drove me back to town so I could pick up my rental. Peters stopped a couple blocks away, on a dark street.

"You sure you shouldn't just head back to L.A.?" Peters said.

"I'm not sure of anything at this point," I said. "But thanks for your help."

"Don't thank us yet," Peters said.

I got out and walked to the corner of the main drag, where I could see Jank's Bar. The motorcycle was gone. There wasn't anybody outside.

I got to my car without running into anyone. Seven minutes

later I pulled in behind the Best Value Motel, parked, and went to my room.

I stopped when I saw the door was ajar.

You've got three choices in a situation like this. Walk in and ask what the heck? But if the heck is a guy, or guys, with guns—which at this point I couldn't rule out—then the open door could be an invitation to get blasted. Or conked over the head.

If you can secure your own weapon, a little shock-and-awe entry could work. Of course, if it wasn't guys with guns in there, but a cleaning lady, you'd spike her heart.

Or you could sit back and wait and see who came out.

I wasn't in a waiting mood. I went to Spinoza, lifted the tarp, got a tire iron from the trunk.

I went back to the open door and peeked inside. Light was coming from the bathroom. I could see my duffel on the bed. Some of my clothes were strewn around it.

I heard something clink in the bathroom.

In two seconds I was at the bathroom door, the tire iron ready to slam on the head of—a kid!

Who screamed.

I said, "What are you doing?"

He was maybe twelve, with a backward baseball cap and T-shirt that hung loosely on his frame. His eyes were as big as manhole covers.

"Don't hit me!" he said, putting his hands up.

"What are you doing in here?"

"Nothin'!"

"That won't fly. Talk to me." I kept the tire iron raised.

"Nothin'. Honest!"

"You're a bad liar. Tell me how you got in."

"The door was already open."

"What do you do? Go around checking doors?"

He shrugged.

"Where you from?" I said. "You live around here?"

"Just let me go," he said.

"You're not going anywhere. You're going to sit down and talk to me."

His eyes gave him away. He tried to run past me. I caught him by the T-shirt and lifted him off the ground. He weighed about as much as my duffel. I carried him out of the bathroom and stuck him on the one chair in the room. I shut the door, turned on the light and sat on the edge of the bed, putting myself between the kid and the door.

"You know what breaking and entering is?" I said.

"I didn't break anything," he said.

"You broke the law."

"I didn't take anything!"

"You took the sanctity of a man's living quarters."

"Huh?"

"What's your name?"

He looked at the floor.

"My name's Mike," I said. "I want to know how you got in here. You're saying the door was open. I locked it when I left. How do you explain that?"

"It was. I swear."

"Do you know what perjury is?"

He shook his head.

"It's when you swear to tell the truth, then don't. And you know what happens if you don't tell the truth after you swear?"

Shook his head again.

"Your guts get lit on fire. You can't sleep. And when you do sleep, you have nightmares. And you stop growing. You'll always be five feet tall, if you're lying."

"Please, just let me go."

Outside my door, a woman's voice shouted, "Joshie!"

"Mom!" The kid jumped out of the chair. Someone tried to open the door. Then knocked on it, hard.

"Joshie, are you in there?"

"Yeah, Mom!"

"Open this door!"

"He won't let me!"

"Who?"

Now a pounding on the door.

With a sigh, I got up and opened the door. A woman of forty or so, with a face full of worry lines, looked me up and down.

"What is...Joshie! Are you all right?"

Joshie flew to his mother, who threw a protective arm around him.

"What is going on here?" She gave me the death glare.

"Your son broke into my room," I said.

"Did not!" Joshie said, with the conviction of a career politician.

"I want the truth," Mom said to me.

"Your little boy is lying," I said. "I caught him going through my stuff. I want to know why."

"Joshie, is that true?" Mom said.

"No!" Joshie said. "He told me to come in."

"Did he touch you?"

"Yes!"

Mom's face turned into a horror show.

"He tried to run out," I said. "I caught him by the shirt and sat his butt in a chair. That's it. Tell Mommy that's the way it was, Joshie."

"No!" Joshie said.

"How did I touch you, Joshie?" I said.

"Well you..." His hesitation lost him the high ground.

"Joshie?" Mom said.

The boy said nothing.

"I don't know what to believe," Mom said.

"I'm willing to bet this isn't the first time little Joshie has lied to you," I said. "The only question is why you let him get away with it."

That hit her. She was stuck now between the rock of reality and the hard place of wanting to protect her boy.

"Look, ma'am," I said. "I'm willing to overlook this if your son will just tell me how he got inside and what he was doing."

"Joshie?" Mom said.

"The door was open and I looked inside," Joshie said. "That's all."

"Why did you think you could go in?" I said.

He shrugged.

"Answer him," Mom said.

Joshie didn't answer. He ran away like a scared jackrabbit.

"I'm sorry," Mom said, rubbing her eyes. "Sometimes I just don't know what to do with him."

"Is there a father in the picture?" I asked.

She shook her head.

"All right," I said. "Let's just forget it. Keep after him about the lying thing. Nip it in the bud, or one day you'll wake up to a horror beyond your imagining. He could become a United States Senator."

That didn't get the laugh I intended.

Mom went to look for Joshie. I went to the front desk.

"Tim," I said, "I just caught a kid in my room, and he says my door was open."

"What!"

"Exactly. Was somebody in there cleaning it or something?"

He looked around and picked up a sheet of paper. "Let's see, housekeeping schedule. Looks like Inez. You want to talk to her?"

"Yeah."

"She's gone now," Tim said. "Want me to give her a call?"

"I'd rather talk to her face to face," I said. "When will she be in?"

"Tomorrow afternoon," Tim said. "Around one."

"Don't say anything to her," I said. "I don't want her prepared."

"Wanna hang out?" Tim said.

"Love to, Tim," I lied. "But I've got some business to attend to."

"You always do," he said. "That's why we love having you here at the Best Value."

"It's nice to be wanted," I said.

I went to my room and read some news on my phone. Up in San Francisco a Honduran drug ring was running rampant, taking full advantage of the sanctuary city status. These "Hondos" rose to dominance in the Tenderloin district during the lockdown era. A beautiful system. The cartels make drugs with chemicals from China, transport them to stash houses in Oakland, distribute them to the Hondo dealers, who take the BART commuter train into the city like any other working stiff. It's the American Dream! Except for the business owners in the Tenderloin, who can't attract customers to the neighborhood anymore.

Across the land, in The Bronx, an "unidentified male" randomly attacked a college student. He used a baseball bat, in broad daylight, then walked casually into the subway. It was the casualness that got me. My stomach felt like it was drowning in slime.

I had to stop scrolling. I called Sophie.

"Hey," she said.

"Tell me something normal," I said.

"Normal?"

"Something that happened today, something bland."

"What is this?" she said.

"Humor me," I said. "What did you have for breakfast?"

"Are you kidding?"

"Eggs? Cereal? Toast."

"I had scrambled eggs. And a croissant. And coffee."

"That's nice," I said.

"Mike, are you okay?"

"Living the dream," I said.

"Yeah?"

"Doing the awesome."

"Okay, now I want you to tell me what is really up."

"I just wanted to hear your voice," I said.

"I'm glad," she said. "And I'm glad to hear yours. But it sounds a little down."

She was getting to know Romeo after all. "I'll tell you what it's like," I said. "I feel like I'm standing in the Roman Forum in 410 A.D., as the Visigoths sack the city."

"Whoa."

"Yeah."

After a pause, she said, "I know what you mean. Things are pretty dismal. Which is why we can't give up."

"No?"

"For the children," she said.

"That's one of my rules," I said.

"That's why I said it."

I put my hand out, as if to touch hers. "I'll be back and we'll fight together."

"I wouldn't have it any other way," she said.

Early next morning, I picked up a sumptuous McDonald's breakfast and drove to where the old lady lived. I found a spot to park about fifty yards away, where I could watch and munch and not draw attention. I was in front of a sandy lot. There was another one at the side of her house. The house across the street from hers didn't have any cars in front of it.

My Egg McMuffin tasted like it had been cooked last night. The coffee was passable.

After an hour I was in a sour mood. My stomach was not much better. This is the romance of surveillance. This whole thing was a hail Mary. That made me think of Noel Auden. I wondered if she had been imploring the Blessed Virgin. I could see her clutching her beads and making supplication on bended knee. I wanted her to know the truth. But that meant I had to find it, and it wasn't exactly sitting up and waving at me. I could almost hear it laughing at me, howling from somewhere out in the desert, like a coyote, and every time I got close it scampered away to another hiding place.

Just as I was considering whether to give it up, an old Ford Crown Victoria backed out of the driveway of the old lady's house. An elderly woman was driving. She drove off, away from my position. I had my Joey Feint picklock kit with me. I jogged over to the house.

I started with the garage. There was a side door with an old fashioned knob lock and a bolt. The bolt took me about a minute. The knob lock was nothing. I went in. A little sunlight through a yellow window pane provide a dim illumination. This was definitely a dwelling, as Officer Peters suggested. There was a mattress on the floor with a pillow and a blanket. A little stove unit was in one corner.

A double-barreled shotgun was mounted on the wall next to the door.

Interesting.

On the floor next to the mattress was a stack of books. Medical books, of all things.

Gross Anatomy
The Big Picture: Physiology
Wound Diagnosis

Forensic Evidence in Criminal Trials

What was this? Some med student living cheap in a garage?

Next to the stack was a black security box, with a lock. No problem at all to pick it. Inside the box were a couple of red binders. I took the top one out and opened it.

There are things you can't unsee. And some of those things will haunt you forever. They'll creep into your mind deep in the night and shake you from your sleep. They'll take whatever hope you have for humanity and toss it in hell's blender.

The binder had print photos, in plastic sleeves. Page after page of children doing things no child should ever be forced to do.

I smacked the binder closed and threw it against the wall. I looked around for a gas can. I was ready to torch the place. But then some cogs started clicking in my mind. And I realized I wanted the guy who lived here, face to face. Because at last something began to make sense.

Now all he had to do was arrive.

Not too much later, he did. I sat on an overturned painter's bucket and waited for the door to open.

It opened.

I was most interested in what his face would do. Eloi Kuprin showed no fear or fright. Just shock, followed by a quick switch to determination. He was quicker than I thought, as he grabbed the shotgun.

And pointed it at me.

"What are you going to do, Ansel?" I said.

"You shouldn't have come here," he said, with perfect voice and diction.

"Why?" I said. "Why kill Steven?"

He grinned. "You'll never know."

"Humor me," I said.

"You're supposed to be so smart."

"All I have to be is smarter than you," I said.

A low, guttural laugh seeped out of his mouth. He sighted down the shotgun and pulled the trigger.

I reached in my pocket and took out the two shells I'd removed earlier.

"Pretty smart, huh?" I said.

He screamed. Yowled like a wild animal. An animal in survival mode. Which made him dangerous with a shotgun-club in his hands.

He charged.

I barely had time to duck and dive. My shoulder hit him in the thighs as the gun butt glanced off my back. He was easy to take down. In two seconds I had him face to the floor, with a neck-crank hold. That's similar to a choke hold. It's illegal in the cage because of the damage it can do.

He gurgled in pain.

"You're going to tell me why you killed Steven Auden," I said. "Or you're going to hell right now."

I let off a little pressure so he could talk.

But he didn't talk. He laughed.

Hysterical, mad laughter.

I choked it off. I almost went too far. I almost wanted to go too far. But I couldn't send him to the infernal regions. He was the only link I had to the truth.

When in doubt, knock them out.

I held the choke until syncope—the temporary loss of consciousness. That takes finesse. I tore up his bed sheet and used the linen to hog-tie him. And gag his mouth.

I called Officer Peters.

"I'm at the old lady's house," I said. "How soon can you get here?"

"What's going on?" Peters said.

"I've got the guy who killed Steven Auden," I said. "He's living in the garage. The old lady's not here right now."

"Tell me what happened."

"You'd better just come," I said.

"Did you break in?"

"Yes."

"Oh, boy."

"You sound like my employer," I said.

"I do?"

"Just get here," I said.

I t took him ten minutes. He and Reed came into the garage. Ansel Foster was breathing slow.

"I got in," I said, "and looked around. His name is Ansel Foster. There's kid porn in those binders, and books on forensic evidence. He used them to figure out how to kill Steven Auden and make it look like suicide."

"Whoa," Officer Reed said.

"He tried to perforate me with that shotgun," I said. "But I took out the shells. He tried to club me. I got him down and here he is."

Reed looked at Peters. Peters scratched his ear.

"He's not talking," I said. "I suggest we wait for the old lady, and you sweat her."

"Sweat her?" Peters said.

"She lied to the sheriff's investigator," I said. "Gave Ansel an alibi for the time of the killing. Let's find out why."

Ansel Foster's scream was muffled by the gag.

"You'd better untie him," Peters said.

"That's not a good idea," I said.

"Let us take it from here."

"Where you going to take it?" I said.

"I'm not sure yet," Peters said.

"Until you do, he stays tied up," I said.

"At least let Officer Reed put cuffs on him."

"With pleasure," I said.

Reed approached Ansel Foster as if he were a Komodo dragon. It did look like he wanted to bite somebody. I waited until she had the bracelets on his wrists, behind his back, before I untied him.

"Keep the gag on him," I said.

"We better take him in," Peters said.

"You have a jail?" I said.

"One cell," Peters said.

I grabbed Ansel's arm and helped Reed get him to his feet. He wanted to struggle. I bent his arms upward. That made him hunch forward and easy to push to the cop car. Peters opened the rear door and I shoved Ansel in.

I said to Peters, "Get a search warrant for the child porn. Make me a confidential informant and eyewitness. But interrogate him on suspicion of murder. I'll give you the facts I know, including his confession."

"Confession?"

"A legit inference," I said. "When I asked him why he killed Steven Auden, he said 'You'll never know.' Then he tried to shoot me."

Peters frowned. "We've got to do this right."

"So far, so good," I said. "Today is Wednesday. You can keep him in jail till Friday afternoon. Then hold him over the weekend. Where are your arraignments?"

"In Imperial. I'll need to talk to the D.A.'s office. And my captain."

"Will that be a problem?" I said.

"I don't know yet," Peters said.

"Why don't you go find out?" I said.

"What are you going to do?"

"Officer Reed and I will stay and keep the scene secure," I said.

"Yeah," Reed said. "That's what we'll do."

"Keep your phone handy," Peters said. He got in the squad car and drove off.

Five minutes later, the old lady pulled in.

In Irish folklore, the banshee is a disembodied spirit in the form of a woman, from the Gaelic *ban sith*—woman of the fairies. When someone is close to death, she appears in the night sky with a mournful scream.

Thus the phrase *screamed like a banshee.*

As the old lady was doing emerging from her car.

She was wraith-like, and her white hair a bird's nest after a storm. The plain, blue dress she wore looked like it hadn't been washed in weeks.

I half expected her to float toward us, like the ghost in the library in *Ghostbusters.*

Instead, she ran toward the house. She moved faster than I thought she could, screaming all the way. She unlocked the front door, went in, slammed it shut.

Reed and I went to the door. Reed knocked.

Nothing.

Another knock, then she said, "Police, ma'am. We need to talk to you."

Not a sound.

Reed turned to me. "Nothing more I can do."

"Shall I unlock the door?"

"No!"

"How about this?" I said.

I pounded on the door a couple of times and said, "We know you lied to the law, lady. You're complicit in a murder. If you talk now it will go easier on you. This house is secured. We're getting a search warrant."

No response.

I turned to Reed. "What would you suggest?"

"We wait," she said.

"Good plan," I said.

There was one tree in the yard, a rosewood, that offered a modicum of shade. Officer Reed and I stood under it.

"I hope we're doing the right thing," Reed said.

"We've got a confessed murderer in custody," I said. "That's a good first step."

"The confession sounds a little iffy. I mean, he wasn't advised of his rights or anything."

"He wasn't in police custody when he said it," I said. "I'm not a cop, either. He wasn't even coerced. He had a shotgun on me. He thought he was golden. We've got an accessory in the house. Somebody's going to crack."

"You called him Ansel Foster," Reed said.

"Ansel Foster is supposed to be dead," I said. "Instead, here he was, playing Claudius."

"Who?"

"There's a book called *I, Claudius*, by Robert Graves," I said. "Claudius was the emperor of Rome between a couple of real winners, Caligula and Nero. He was thought to be a harmless dolt because he limped and had a speech impediment. He was actually smart and scheming. So here was Ansel, hiding in plain sight, pretending to be an idiot."

"And you think he shot the student and made it look like suicide?"

"I'm sure of it," I said. "The only question is why. That old lady in there probably knows."

"This is so weird," Reed said.

"What is?"

"This whole thing. I mean, not that somebody committed a murder. That happens everywhere. But that somebody could be hiding out like that."

"There's no shortage of weird in the annals of crime," I said. "There was a case in Los Angeles way back in the 1920s, where a married woman hid a little man in her attic for years, having trysts with him when her husband went to work. The husband had no idea. When they moved, the wife insisted on finding a house with an attic. The husband didn't know why, but went along with it. She moved the little man into the new house."

"Yeah, that is weird."

"One day the little guy heard the husband and wife arguing. He thought he needed to come rescue her. Down he came, his skin yellow from never being in the sun. The husband pulled a gun. There was a struggle, and the husband ends up dead."

"Whoa," Reed said.

"But nobody knew the little man lived in the attic. And get this, he wanted to be a pulp fiction writer. That's all he read, pulp magazines. So he cooked up a story. The wife and husband were subject to a burglar, who shot the husband and locked the wife in a closet. So in the closet she went, and screamed until somebody got her out. The D.A. wanted to try the wife for murder, but her lawyer pointed out that she'd been locked in the closet from the outside. Case dismissed."

"They got away with it?"

"The wheels of justice turn slowly, but grind exceedingly fine."

"What?"

"Justice catches up eventually. Most of the time, at least. Years later they found the little man, he confessed, and was charged with manslaughter. But the statute of limitations had run out, and he walked."

"What about the wife?"

"Hung jury. She walked, too, and lived another thirty years."

"With the little man?"

I shook my head. "He left L.A. and was never heard of again."

"Hm, doesn't seem like justice was served."

"That's my job," I said.

"Huh?"

"I'm a justice grinder."

Reed smiled. "You're an interesting guy."

"I've been called worse," I said.

Twenty more minutes went by. No word from Peters about a warrant. I was starting to get antsy.

A squeal of tires on the road. A black Lexus turned into the driveway and skidded to a stop. A woman in a business suit got out. She had black hair pulled back so hard it looked like it was giving her a face lift. She was in her early thirties and would have looked like a homecoming queen if she smiled. But her mouth was a steel trap. It snapped open to say, "You will both clear out. You're trespassing."

Officer Reed said, "This is a crime scene."

"It is not," the woman said.

"Explain yourself," I said.

"I'm here on behalf of the home owner," she said. "And you are harassing her."

"Do you see the police officer here?" I said.

"We're waiting for a search warrant," Reed said.

"There will be no warrant," the woman said. "I suggest you call your captain. And then leave."

Reed looked at me. She took out her phone.

As she made the call, I said to the buzz saw, "Lawyer?"

She just looked at me.

I said, "You might want to inform your client that she's under suspicion of being an accessory to murder, and it would go better for her if she talked to us."

This finally brought a smile to the woman's face. The smug

kind. "It will go better for you, Mr. Romeo, if you vacate the premises."

Officer Reed came over to me. Her face was drained of color.

"The cap wants to see us," she said.

"Good idea," Buzz Saw said.

To Buzz Saw I said, "You're not from around here. Too fancy. Think too much of yourself. National firm with an office in San Diego, I'd say."

"You're out of your league," Buzz Saw said. "Take the L and go back to Los Angeles."

"You haven't seen my fastball yet."

"I'm shaking."

"I'm just getting warmed up."

The smugness on her face was a neon sign that told me she billed at $1,000 an hour.

"If you want to play," she said, "I'll be waiting."

R eed didn't have any information to offer as I drove her to the Moreland police station. All she would say is that it didn't sound good.

The station was in a modest brown building that looked like it had once been a department store. Through the front door was a reception area with no one at the desk. I followed Reed down a hallway to an open door at the end.

Officer Peters was sitting in a chair. At the desk was a man in his fifties who had enjoyed a few too many cheeseburgers in this time.

"This is the guy?" the man said. There was a name plate on his desk that read, *Capt. Gene Walton.*

Peters said, "Yes, sir."

Walton stood. "I'm wondering what to charge you with."

"Charge *me*?" I said.

"You want to tell me why you're breaking into private residences?"

"Didn't Officer Peters here tell you what happened?"

"He sure did."

"So where is the prisoner?" I said. "I can tell you the charge, murder of a young man named Steven Auden. And attempted murder of yours truly."

"Close the door," Walton said to Reed. She did. To me he said, "Have a seat."

"No," I said.

"Have it your way," Walton said.

"I usually do," I said. "Have you questioned Ansel Foster yet?"

"There's not going to be any questioning. Except of you."

I looked at Peters. "Can you tell me what's going on here? Didn't you explain things to him?"

Peters didn't say anything. He looked at the floor.

"Where's Foster?" I said.

Peters looked at Walton. Walton looked at me. Reed didn't seem to know who to look at.

"You let him go," I said.

"There is nothing to hold him on," Walton said.

"Didn't Officer Peters tell you he confessed to me about killing Steven Auden?"

"That was no confession," Walton said. "It was an ambiguous statement. Who knows what he meant? You broke into his residence. You beat him up. You're the one who needs to be locked up."

"You let him get away," I said. "Who knows where he's gone? Frank Foster is lawyering up, for the old lady and no doubt his son. Doesn't that set off any alarm bells?"

"No," Walton said.

"What kind of a clown show is this place?" I said.

"You want to leave or do I throw you in jail?" Walton said.

"You're the Red Queen," I said.

He looked blank.

"Sentence first, verdict afterward," I said. "Off with some heads."

"This is getting us nowhere," Walton said.

"We're already nowhere," I said.

I turned to leave.

"Where are you going?" Walton said.

"To do some grinding," I said.

"Stop right there."

I kept walking.

Nobody came after me. That's when I knew Walton hadn't checked to see if I had an outstanding arrest warrant via the county sheriff.

I was so steamed I was dizzy. My head was a hive of killer bees buzzing angrily after being poked by a stick. I'd had him! Ansel Foster, killer, and now he was gone, home to the arms of Papa, who had the money and means to hide him again.

I burned some rubber back to Roethke. Tomeka, the original receptionist, was at the front desk. I spooked her little by approaching like mad bull.

"I need to see Dr. Susa," I said.

She took a deep breath. "I'm sorry," she said. "He's not in."

"Where is he?"

"He's been hurt."

"Hurt?"

She nodded.

"How bad?" I said.

"It's so awful." Her eyes were moistening. "Why does this happen?"

"Why don't you tell me what happened?"

"Somebody attacked him in his home, at night," Tomeka said.

"Robbery?"

Tomika shook her head.

"Where is he now?" I said.

"I really shouldn't say."

"This is about Eloi Kuprin," I said.

"Eloi? Is he all right?"

"He is not," I said. "I need to ask Dr. Susa about it."

"What's wrong?"

"Tomeka, who would have been the one to hire Eloi?"

She frowned. "I don't know."

"Dr. Susa?"

She moved uncomfortably in her chair.

I said, "Do this for me. Call him. Tell him I'm here and I need to see him. Will you do that for me?"

"This is very upsetting."

"Hang in there," I said. "I'll wait."

She hesitated, then picked up the phone and punched a speed dial number.

"There's no answer," she said.

"Leave a message," I said. "Tell him to call me." I grabbed a Sticky Note from the reception desk and a pen, and wrote my number on it.

"Thank you," I said.

"Can you protect him?" Tomeka said.

"Who?"

"Eloi. He's so vulnerable."

"I'll see what I can do," I said.

When I went into the lobby of the Best Value, Troubadour Tim had the TV going. Clint Eastwood was squinting and smiling, gun in hand.

"Listen, Troubadour—"

He put his hand up to silence me. Clint Eastwood said, "I know what you're thinking. Did he fire six shots or only five? Well to tell you the truth in all this excitement I kinda lost track myself. But being this is a .44 Magnum, the most powerful handgun in the world, and would blow your head clean off, you've gotta ask yourself one question—Do I feel lucky? Well, do ya, punk?"

"I love this movie," Tim said.

"*Dirty Harry*," I said. "Classic."

"You like it, too?"

"What's not to like?"

Tim hit the mute button and turned to me. "I think I know who left your door open."

"Do tell," I said.

"His name's Javier. He's fifteen. Son of one of my cleaning ladies, Inez. He's trouble. I've chased him out of here a few times."

"Where can I find him?"

"No idea. Maybe he's at his mom's."

"Can you find out?"

"I guess we could ask her."

"Let's."

Tim looked at the wall clock. "She should be here in half an hour. Why don't you hang out?"

"You have a good hang out spot?"

"Right here. I could try out a couple of new songs on you."

"I just remembered I have to check my messages," I said.

"You could hang out by the pool," Tim said.

"Your pool has no water."

"That means nobody'll crowd you."

I tapped my head with my index finger. "Good thinking, Tim."

He smiled.

I did go out by the pool. The air was hot and dry. A young couple with two little kids came out of one of the rooms. The adults carried suitcases. The kids—a boy and a girl—wore little backpacks. The girl's backpack was pink. The boy's was green. I thought I saw ninja turtles on the boy's backpack. I smiled. The male instinct to fight and protect was still intact. At least it was here, for the moment, in a small town in the desert. Fight on, kid. Keep standing up for yourself. They'll try to take away your spirit someday. Don't let 'em.

Time passed. I fell asleep. Then heard Tim's voice calling me to come to the office.

S he was a short, stocky woman in a faded blue housekeeping uniform.

"This is Inez Herrera," Tim said. "I told her you wanted to talk to her."

She looked at me with frightened brown eyes.

"I was wondering if I might talk to your son," I said.

In a thick accent, she said, "You are police?"

"No, no. I'm a guest. My room door was open when I got back here. I'm trying to find out why."

Tim said, "Inez, you're not in trouble. Mr. Romeo isn't interested in pressing charges. He just wants to find out why it may have happened."

Inez Herrera looked at her hands. "No trouble?"

"No trouble," I said.

"I try with him," she said, shaking her head. "But the drugs. *Muy malo.*"

"May I talk with him?" I said.

"I do not know," she said.

"Do you know where is now?" Tim said.

She shook her head. "Maybe with friends. *El parque.*"

Tim said, "Kids go there to smoke."

"No trouble," Inez said. She was begging with her eyes. I extended my hand. She took it. I put my other hand on top. "I promise, no trouble."

I shouldn't have promised.

T he park was in the center of town. Made up of green and brown grass with a play area in one corner. The play area had a slide, a set of swings, and a tire hanging from three chains.

No kids were playing there. No dogs were sniffing there. Desolation.

An old man walked across the patchy ground of the park, using a hiking pole.

In a far corner, on a bench, sat two boys, teens it looked like. I made my way over.

When I was twenty yards away they took notice and stiffened. It's illegal to smoke pot in California if you're under twenty-one. Nothing will happen to a scofflaw except maybe attendance at some education class, or a bit of community service like picking up trash and needles. Still, no kid wants that hassle.

One of the boys was white with a blond buzz cut. The other was brown with thick black hair.

"Hello, Javier," I said.

The black-haired boy scowled. "Who're you?"

"I'm the guy whose room you broke into."

It took one second for him to jump up and run.

H e was fleet of foot. But all my running in the sand at Paradise Cove was good training for such a time as this. I chased him half way across the park and got him by the back of the shirt.

He wriggled like a mackerel.

"Lemme go!"

"Calm down," I said.

"Let him go, man." It was the other kid. He was walking fast toward us. He flipped open a butterfly knife.

I pulled Javier around so he was between me and the knife kid.

"Don't do that," I said. "Someday a guy like me is going to take that from you and do some jigsaw work."

"Just let him go," Knife Kid said.

"How about you walk away before you get hurt?"

I twisted Javier's arm behind him. He squealed.

"Tell him to go away," I said to Javier, "or I dislocate your arm."

Javier said nothing. He tried to writhe out of my hold.

Knife Kid didn't know what to do.

"You want to try me?" I said. "Come on. I'll do you one handed."

I hoped he wouldn't. I don't like to hurt kids.

He said, "What do you want me to do, Javi?"

I pulled his arm, getting a yelp.

"Just go," Javier said.

Knife Kid looked at me and flipped his blade closed. "This isn't over," he said.

"Oh, it's over," I said.

He spat on the ground. Then walked away.

"This doesn't have to be hard," I said to Javier. "If I let you go and you try to run again, I'll disconnect some joints. Got it?"

"What are you gonna do to me?" he said.

"Just talk. Okay?"

"Lemme go."

"Sure."

I gave him his arm back.

He said, "What's your deal, man?"

"My deal? You're the one who broke into my room."

"I didn't do nothin'."

"Javi. May I call you Javi?"

"No."

"Javi, you know that running away is a sign of consciousness of guilt, right?"

"Huh?"

"It mean you're a bad liar, Javi. It's going to get you into a lot of trouble one of these days."

"Whatta you want from me?"

"I just want to know why you were in my room. Why you abused your mother's employment to gain access. Why you put her job in jeopardy."

He kicked some dirt.

"Money?" I said. "Money for drugs?"

"Just leave me alone," Javier said.

"How old are you?"

He said nothing.

"Fifteen?"

He shrugged.

"You want to make it to sixteen? Or eighteen?"

"Who cares?"

"You don't care about dying?"

"Everybody dies," he said.

"You want your mother to die? Because that's what you're doing to her. You're killing her slowly. You care about that?"

He looked at the ground.

"You already know the answer," I said. "But you won't listen. Because you've cooked your brain and seared your conscience."

"I don't know what you're sayin'!"

"If it was money you were after, just tell me."

"So what?"

"It's called stealing, that's so what. You steal from the wrong guy someday, and yeah, you'll get your wish and die, and your mom will get to mourn you."

"Okay! I went for money, but you didn't have any. So now what?"

"If I thought you'd do right by your mom, I'd let you go," I said.

"You would?"

"Don't you think you owe her?"

His face clenched. There was something going on behind his eyes. Something good trying to get out.

"Okay," he said.

"Anything else you want to tell me?"

He hesitated, the said, "There's talk about you. They know who you are."

"Who does?"

"Guys you don't want to mess with," he said. "I don't know names. They hang out together."

"Ride motorcycles, maybe?"

"Yeah."

"Anything else you can tell me about these guys?"

He shook his head.

"All right, Javi. You can go. Just remember to think about your mom."

At least he nodded before he walked away.

S tanding there in the open park, I felt like a tin can on the fence at a shooting range. I found myself wishing for some of Ira's Old Testament justice. For heavenly armies or the Angel of the Lord to come down to Morland with flaming swords.

But as I told C Dog, if wishes were horses, beggars would ride.

Turns out, though, that Ira himself rode to the rescue.

· · ·

I was back in my room at the motel, wondering what to do next and coming up with, well, bupkis.

Ira called. "Where are you now, Michael?"

"The eighth circle of hell ," I said.

"Is that the one with the harpies?" Ira said.

"No, it's the one with Simon Magus and the bad popes, buried upside down, with his feet sticking out and flames burning them for eternity."

"Oh, is that all?" Ira said. "You're ready for a change."

"What do you have in mind?"

"Temecula. It's about two hours away."

"Yeah, I've read the brochures," I said. "What's in Temecula besides wine?"

"Albert Staley," Ira said.

"You found him?"

"I found his house," Ira said. "How's your car holding up?"

"I'm using a rental," I said.

"What's wrong with Spinoza?"

"Nothing," I said. "He just needed some time off to work on the problem of infinite substance. I'm working on a different set of problems." I told him about Eloi-Ansel, the child porn, the smug lawyer. "They got Ansel out. Who knows where they'll hide him?"

"I know someone who might be able to help."

"Who?"

"David Becker."

"The guy with the special ops team?"

"What team?" Ira said.

"Call him," I said.

T emecula is a popular spot for weekend getaways and winery tours, with good food, farmer's markets, and even hot-air balloons. The friendly homes favor Spanish-style roofs and palm trees.

The home Ira found was of modest size, tucked into a cul-de-sac. It was stucco and brick, with a lush green lawn and manicured shrub of silver lupine. Nice place. Someone could be happy here.

But the man who answered my knock did not look happy. He was late forties, with thinning brown hair.

"Albert Staley?" I said.

His eyes narrowed. "Who are you?"

"My name is Mike Romeo," I said.

"What do you want?"

"I'm not here to sell anything," I said. "I was hoping you might help me on a matter of some importance. I work for a lawyer in Los Angeles, and we represent the mother of young man named Steven Auden. Would you mind if I—"

"I don't know anyone by that name." He started to shut the door. I hadn't come this far to be put off. The old salesman-foot-in-the-door trick worked.

"What are you doing?" he said.

"I need to talk to you, Mr. Staley," I said, and pushed my way in.

"You can't come in!"

"You moved here from El Centro. Steven Auden was going to school in Morland, at the Roethke Spiritual Center. He seems to have known you."

"You have no right to come in here."

"Maybe I do," I said.

"I have nothing to say to you."

"You are Albert Staley, yes?"

"I'm not going to answer any questions. Leave now, or I will call the police."

"Why don't you do that?" I said.

"What?"

I went for the direct approach. "I'll tell them about your complicity in the murder of Steven Auden."

He put his hand on his chest. All breath seemed to leave him.

"So you did know him," I said.

"Dear God." He leaned back against the wall. "Why do you say murder?"

"Because it wasn't suicide."

"And you think I...how could you?"

"You tell me," I said.

He took a couple deep breaths. Finally he said, "You don't understand. I can't talk to you. I can't tell you anything."

"Can't or won't?"

"Please go away," he said. "We've had enough trouble."

"We?"

He said nothing.

"What aren't you telling me?" I said.

His eyes pleaded with me. I wasn't in a softhearted mood. I was just about to press him again when a woman's voice said, "We need to tell him, Daddy."

She was standing at the other end of the entryway. She was slight, with soft brown hair draping over her shoulders. In the muted light she could have been sixteen or thirty or anywhere in between.

"No," Albert Staley said.

The young woman approached me.

"You knew Steven?" I said.

She nodded.

"We need to talk to a lawyer," Albert Staley said.

"I'm close enough," I said.

The woman said, "Why do you say Steven was murdered?"

"It's what the evidence suggests," I said. "And your father's name came up in a conversation Steven had with a reporter. I'm here to find out why."

She looked at her father. "We have to tell him."

Albert Staley closed his eyes. "All right."

"May I know your name?" I asked.

"Rebecca," she said.

S ometimes, little things blow up into big things.

The assassination of Julius Caesar was a big thing. It left two of his kinsmen in charge of Rome. One was Octavian, Caesar's grand-nephew and adopted heir. The other was Mark Antony, distantly related through his mother, to Caesar. They got together with a fellow named Lepidus and formed a triumvirate to decide the fate of the Roman territories. But the two main guys were rivals, and civil war almost broke out. To settle things down, Antony married Octavian's sister.

But then Antony fell for an Egyptian vixen named Cleopatra. So he divorced his wife. This Octavian did not care for. He declared Antony a traitor. Antony and Cleo tried to defeat Octavian's army, but failed. As a result, they committed suicide. Which shows that divorce can be hazardous to your health.

And that a man's uncontrolled passion for sexual conquest can blow up an empire.

All of which was going through my mind as I showed up, unannounced, at Nicolas Susa's house on a tree-lined street in Brawley.

My first few knocks were met with silence.

"Need to talk, Dr. Susa," I said, and knocked again.

He opened the door. He had two black eyes and tape across his nose.

"What is it you want?" he said.

I pushed the door and went inside. I was getting good at this.

"Wait!" Susa said.

"You've had a little trouble," I said.

"No thanks to you," he said.

"Me?"

"This happened because of your snooping around," he said.

"You're going to have to explain that one."

"I cooperated with you fully. Because of that someone was made unhappy, and a fellow showed up here to tell me not to talk with you any further. He did this to me for emphasis."

"What did this fellow look like?"

"I don't know," Susa said. "He wore a ski mask. And you've brought negative energy to our campus that is being manifested upon innocent parties. Please go away."

The living room was off to the right. I walked in. It had soft tones and plants and a small fireplace. Susa scurried in behind me.

"Now wait a minute," he said.

"Maybe you'd better sit down," I said.

"Do not tell me what to do," he said.

"Sit."

"I will not."

"Eloi Kuprin," I said.

"What about him?"

"He's not Eloi Kuprin," I said. "He's Ansel Foster, and he killed Steven Auden."

Susa put his hands on his hips. "What did you just say?"

"You got negative energy in your ears?" I said.

"This is bizarre," Susa said. "And who is Ansel Foster?"

"I think you know," I said. I waited for his cheeks to twitch. They did.

"Maybe now you should sit down," I said.

He thought a moment, then sat in a chair by the fireplace.

"Make it fast," he said. "I have a radio interview coming up."

"Should be interesting," I said. "Maybe you can tell them about Rebecca Staley."

Another twitch in his cheeks. But he kept his eyes steady. "Who is that?"

"Too late, Susa," I said. "We found her. And she's going to talk."

Now his eyes betrayed a churning in the brain. I could almost hear the meshing and grinding of the gears. His bliss was seriously messed up.

All he came up with was, "I have no idea what you're talking about."

"Then let me start with your face," I said. "Did you ever see *Dirty Harry*?"

"What on earth does that have to do with anything?"

"Humor me. Have you ever seen it?"

"Maybe years ago," he said. "I can't remember."

"That's a pretty clumsy lie," I said. "Nobody forgets *Dirty Harry*."

"Will you get to the point?"

"The bad guy in the movie, a real psycho, hires a street thug to beat his face in. Then he tells the press that Harry did this to him. It was a way to shift suspicion. I have a feeling that's what you did. Had a guy hit you a few times, make you look like a victim instead of a suspect. You felt the walls coming down."

"What walls?"

"The walls of Jericho."

"You're talking myth now," Susa said.

"I'm about to blow the trumpet," I said. "Rebecca Staley was seventeen years old when you raped her. You bought her and her father off with a nice sum of money and an NDA. You hired Wiley Gant to threaten them should they ever break the agreement. How am I doing so far?"

He just looked at me.

I said, "Steven Auden met Rebecca doing odd jobs for her father. They became close. They kept in touch, even after she moved to Temecula. Steven picked up that something was wrong, and Rebecca finally told him in confidence, and never to tell. That didn't sit well with Steven. He was preparing to get the story out anonymously. Eloi Kuprin—I mean Ansel Foster—got wind of this. I don't know exactly how. Maybe he overheard something. Or maybe he hacked into Steven's laptop when he wasn't around. Then someone came up with the idea of staging a suicide. Might have been you. Or maybe there was another—"

"*EEEEE!*"

A scream pierced my brain. I turned just in time to see—

—a Viking with a battle axe, charging at me.

I had one second to make the right move or get sliced in half.

D ísir held the axe in her right hand, arm at shoulder level. Instinct told me she was going to side-arm it into my neck.

I flopped on my back.

The blade whooshed over me.

I stomp-kicked Dísir's right knee so hard it cracked.

She wailed like a pig on a pike.

I crunched to a sitting position, grabbed her axe arm at the wrist. I yanked. Her bum leg couldn't resist. Down she came.

I punched her in the face.

She was out. I got up and took the axe from her hand. The Vikings were known for their mastery of this weapon of war. Meant to be wielded with one hand, it had a teakwood handle with leather strips around it, and a hooked blade.

I held it up as I faced Susa.

"I swear I didn't tell them to do it!" he said. "They killed Steven and held it over my head. Said they'd keep it quiet if I cooperated. I didn't know Eloi was Ansel Foster until after Steven's death. Dísir is the one who hired him."

"Why?"

"Because she and Frank Foster are…"

"Lovers?"

"It's complicated," Susa said.

"Try me," I said.

"You saw her with the axe," Susa said. "Imagine what she can do with whips and—"

"That'll do," I said.

Dísir moaned.

"Listen," I said. "You have to choose now. If you cooperate, we can help you. Me and my lawyer employer. If you don't, you will no doubt land in prison. You know what they do to rapists in prison?"

"I can't go to prison. I can't!"

"They may let you have your otters," I said.

That's when Nicolas Susa began to weep.

"Cut it out," I said. "Do you have any duct tape?"

"What?"

"Duct tape."

"Ye...yes."

"Show me."

Wiping his eyes with the back of his hand, Susa went to a cabinet in his laundry room. He handed me a big spool of what no home should be without.

We went back to the living room.

"Sit down and be quiet," I said.

I took the woozy Viking princess and put her in a straight-backed chair. I taped her to the chair until she began to resemble a mummy.

And came to her senses. What poured out of her mouth then was a stream of curses, both ancient and modern. She called down the gods of Valhalla on us, threatened Susa with flaming death, told me I'd be sent to *Niflheimr*—hell in Norse mythology.

So I taped her mouth shut.

And then placed a call to Officer Mal Peters.

.   .   .

A s we waited, Désir wiggled and moaned. I could almost hear the F bombs through the tape.

Susa motioned for me. Softly, he said, "Isn't there some way I can get out of this? You and I could work together."

"On what?" I said.

"A story," Susa said.

"This story has to end with you paying a price," I said.

"What price?"

"Well, Oprah won't be returning your calls. I doubt you'll get a PBS show."

"I'll have nothing," he said.

"You'll have your life," I said. "Some of the best stories are about restoration. Samson was a fool, got a bad haircut, lost his strength, was blinded by his enemies. But he got one last chance to be a hero and killed a bunch of Philistines."

"But he died, too."

"It's not a perfect analogy," I said.

"I'm not feeling any better."

"Ask me if I care about your feelings," I said.

He lowered his head. "What do I do now?"

Désir made a sound like a muffled scream.

"Do you have a hall closet?" I said.

T wenty minutes later I answered the knock at the door. Officer Peters was there with his captain, Walton.

"This way," I said.

They followed me to the living room where Nicolas Susa was still sitting in the chair by the fireplace.

"Okay," Walton said. "What's this about?"

"This is Dr. Nicolas Susa," I said. "Dean of the Roethke Spiritual Center. He's got some things to tell. He's being represented by a legal team, of which I am a part."

"A team?"

I gave him one of Ira's cards.

"All right," Walton said. "So what's he supposed to have done?"

"First of all, he's a witness to attempted murder," I said.

"Of who?"

"Me."

"Oh, yeah?" Walton said. "Who tried to kill you?"

"See that axe?" I said.

He looked. "So?"

"Somebody almost cut me in two with it."

"Who?"

"You'll find her in the hall closet."

Walton scowled. He said to Peters, "Go check it out."

Peters walked out.

"This is sounding really screwy," Walton said.

"Oh, it gets screwier," I said. "It's also the biggest bust in the history of Morland. The kind of bust that can make a reputation, if it's handled right."

"You think that's what I think about?"

"All men do," I said.

Peters came back. "Um, there's a woman in the closet wrapped in duct tape."

"She's the one who tried to kill me," I said. "Dr. Susa saw the whole thing. He will also tell you that she's complicit in the murder of Steven Auden, the student at Roethke who was ruled a suicide."

He looked at Susa. "That so?"

Susa nodded.

"So why don't you have Officer Peters here take the Viking assassin to your jail cell," I said. "And set up a meeting with the D.A.'s office."

· · ·

W alton and Peters had fun getting Dísir out of her bonds and into handcuffs. She writhed and kicked. Her face was purple and puffy where I socked her. When they took the tape off her mouth, the explosion of profanity sounded like a beer-soaked melee in a waterfront dive. But as long as they didn't question her, anything she spouted could be used against her in court. She was doing a lot of spouting as Peters drove away.

Walton made a call to the D.A., and I called Ira. I filled him in on my recent brush with death. He gave me his standard "Hoo boy" and then we discussed how to negotiate immunity for Nicolas Susa.

Which was done two hours later at the Morland Police station. A deputy D.A. from the Imperial office came up from El Centro. We got Ira on Zoom and worked out a plea deal for Nicolas Susa to talk.

And talk he did.

I t was twilight when I got back to my motel. I bid goodbye to Troubadour Tim. He said he'd call the rental guy to pick up the car, and told me to please come back. I told him not to wait up, but wished him happy songs and lots of loose change at the park.

Then I got in Spinoza and headed home.

With a stop in Temecula to tell Albert Staley and Rebecca what went down.

"It doesn't seem real," Albert Staley said. He was sitting on the sofa with his arm around his daughter.

I said, "I know it's less than ideal that Susa isn't going to prison. I needed his testimony."

Rebecca nodded. "You did it for Steven. And his mother."

"Thank you," I said.

"What about this Ansel Foster?" Albert Staley said.

"I'm sure he'll get picked up soon," I said, though I wasn't sure at all. They sensed it, too. I could see it in their eyes. It's the look we all get when what we long for is out there, just beyond our reach. We want to grab it, but end up with a handful of wind. It's a look that keeps me up at night.

And night it was as I drove back to L.A. Along the way I called I called Kari Innes. She was giddy with excitement at what used to be called a scoop from an "unnamed source." Which is just what I like to be.

T he next day Ira and I went to see Noel Auden. On the way over in Ira's van, I said, "Now is as good a time as any to tell you why Coltrane Smith wanted to talk to me."

"Oh, I know why," Ira said.

"Excuse me?"

"You think I don't know how to hack into LAPD computers? That I couldn't cross-check your description? That it might have something to do with you and your green car? Is that what you think?"

"You did all that?"

"I didn't do any of it," Ira said. "I called Coltrane Smith and asked him to tell me what was going on. Nice fellow."

"And you weren't going to tell me?"

"I was just waiting to see if you told me first," Ira said. "Thank you for being forthright."

"If there is a category called sneaky, too-clever-by-half rabbis," I said, "you're at the top of the list."

"I love you, too," Ira said.

. . .

Noel Auden sat calmly as I gave her all the facts. In spite of the quiet tears she shed, she seemed at peace. Her son had not died a suicide, but as a result of helping someone he cared about.

"That is so like him," she said at last.

She insisted on paying us a fee. Ira finally settled with her on three-hundred dollars. That covered about a quarter of our gas cost. But it was more than enough for us.

I got back to the Cove in the afternoon. I plopped on my futon, wanting nothing more than to listen to the waves for awhile. Instead—

"Hey, man!" C Dog was at the screen door.

"Come on in," I said.

He went to the sofa. "Man, that Shakespeare is hard to get into," he said.

"How far are you?"

"I think I'm in the middle of Act Two," he said.

"Any of it getting through?"

"I get that they really dig each other."

"A scholar could not have put it any more pithily."

"Pithy what?"

"In few words," I said. "But how do you know they dig each other?"

"The way they talk," C Dog said.

"Give me an example," I said.

"Oh...well..."

"The first time he sees her," I said. "What does she teach the torches?"

"Torches?"

"She doth teach the torches to burn bright."

"Uh-huh."

"And what light through yonder window breaks?"

"Light...yeah..."

"It is the east, and Juliet is the sun."

"Yeah, yeah, I remember that. He's really gone."

"That's called love, my friend."

"Cool," he said. "Do I have to finish it?"

"Yes, you have to finish it."

"Aw, man."

"Cry me a river," I said. "I've got to face a class of seventh graders and talk about the play. You want to come with me?"

"No way! You're on your own, dude."

A nd I was. The very next day.

"Everyone, this is my friend, Mike Romeo," Sophie said.

A few giggles bubbled up from the kids in her classroom, twenty strong.

"That's right," Sophie said. "Romeo, as in *Romeo and Juliet*. He's here to talk to us about the play."

My knees jiggled as Sophie sat at her desk, leaving me alone in the front of the room. "We'll talk together," I said. "How did you like the play?"

A girl's hand went up. "I thought it was really sad that they died."

"Yes, you're supposed to feel sad," I said. "That's why it's called a tragedy. Why do you think Shakespeare wrote this as a tragedy?"

They thought about it. But no one raised a hand.

I wished Sophie had assigned *As You Like It*.

"Sometimes life is sad," I said. "That's what a tragedy tells us. But that helps us appreciate the happy parts when they come along."

A few furrowed brows, but no responses.

I cleared my throat. "If you could have met William Shakespeare, what would have been your advice on how to end the play?"

Two quick hands shot up. A boy and a girl. I called on the boy.

"A sword fight," he said. "Romeo could kill some bad guys, then jump on a horse, and go and get Juliet, and then they could ride off to France."

That got some giggles, but some of the other boys nodded in approval.

The girl said, "Couldn't there be a potion that brings them back to life?"

I looked at Sophie then. She smiled. It was a smile that taught the torches to burn bright.

"Sword fights and magic potions," I said. "How's that sound, Miss Montag?"

"I think we've got a hit," Sophie said.

It was two days later that Ira called me with the news that Ansel Foster had been picked up trying to cross into Mexico. He got delivered to an FBI field office, along with a cache of child pornography. How that happened remains a mystery.

To most people, that is. Not to Ira, David Becker, or me.

The FBI also questioned the old lady who put Ansel up in her garage. Turns out she is Ansel Foster's aunt. And mad as a hatter, if you can even find a hatter these days.

After the call I had to go down to the beach. The sun was setting and the sky was burnt orange. The sea shimmered with a shaft of fiery radiance. I just stood there, letting the water ebb and flow over my feet, listening to the waves.

Finally, Sisyphus could catch a breath.

At least for a few hours.

AUTHOR'S NOTE

Many thanks for reading *Romeo's Justice*. I greatly appreciate it. Added appreciation would come if you would kindly leave a review on the Amazon site.

The Mike Romeo Thriller Series
(in order)
1. Romeo's Rules
2. Romeo's Way
3. Romeo's Hammer
4. Romeo's Fight
5. Romeo's Stand
6. Romeo's Town
7. Romeo's Rage
8. Romeo's Justice

FREE BOOK

I'd like to offer you a free suspense novella, FRAMED. You can pick it up by going to my website: JamesScottBell.com. Navigate to the FREE BOOK page and follow the link. Enjoy!

MORE THRILLERS FROM JAMES SCOTT BELL

The Ty Buchanan Legal Thriller Series

#1 Try Dying
#2 Try Darkness
#3 Try Fear

"Part Michael Connelly and part Raymond Chandler, Bell has an excellent ear for dialogue and makes contemporary L.A. come alive. Deftly plotted, flawlessly executed, and compulsively readable. Bell takes his place as one of the top authors in the crowded suspense genre." - **Sheldon Siegel**, *New York Times* bestselling author

The Trials of Kit Shannon Historical Legal Thrillers

Book 1 - City of Angels
Book 2 - Angels Flight
Book 3 - Angel of Mercy
Book 4 - A Greater Glory
Book 5 - A Higher Justice

Book 6 - A Certain Truth

"With her shoulders squared and faith set high, Kit Shannon arrives in 1903 Los Angeles feeling a special calling to practice law ... Packed full of genuine, deep and real characters ... The tension and suspense are in overdrive ... A series that is time-less!" — **In the Library Review**

Stand Alone Thrillers

Your Son Is Alive
Long Lost
Can't Stop Me
No More Lies
Blind Justice
Don't Leave Me
Final Witness
Framed
Last Call

Mallory Caine, Zombie-At-Law Series

You read that right. A new genre. Part John Grisham, part Raymond Chandler—it's just that the lawyer is dead. Mallory Caine, Zombie at Law, defends the creatures no other lawyer will touch...and longs to reclaim her real life.

Pay Me In Flesh
The Year of Eating Dangerously
I Ate The Sheriff

ABOUT THE AUTHOR

 **James Scott Bell** is a multi-best-selling author of thrillers and books on the writing craft. He is a winner of the International Thriller Writers Award, the Christy Award (Suspense), and the ACFW Lifetime Achievement Award. He attended the University of California, Santa Barbara, where he studied writing with Raymond Carver, and graduated with honors from USC Law School. He lives and writes in Los Angeles.

JamesScottBell.com

Printed in Great Britain
by Amazon

28565082R00119